"'MAY YOU HAVE NUFFIN' BUT DE FACES OF FRIEN'S IN IT FU' DE REASON DAT YOU HAS NO INIMIES'"

In Old Plantation Days

By

Paul Laurence Dunbar

ILLUSTRATED

NEGRO UNIVERSITIES PRESS
NEW YORK

Originally published in 1903
by Dodd, Mead, and Company

Reprinted 1969 by
Negro Universities Press
A DIVISION OF GREENWOOD PUBLISHING CORP.
NEW YORK

SBN 8371-1886-7

PRINTED IN UNITED STATES OF AMERICA

CONTENTS

In Old Plantation Days

AUNT TEMPE'S TRIUMPH.

It was in the glow of an April evening when Aunt Tempe came out on the veranda to hold a conference with her master, Stuart Mordaunt. She had evidently been turning some things over in her mind.

For months there had been talk on the plantation, but nobody knew the inside of what was going on quite so well as she, for was she not Miss Eliza's mammy? Had she not cared for her every day of her life, from her birth until now, and was she not still her own child, her "Lammy?"

Indeed, at first she had entirely opposed the marriage of her young mistress to anybody, and had discouraged the attentions of young Stone Daniels when she thought he was "spa'kin' roun' "; but when Miss Eliza laid her head on her breast and blushingly told her all about it she surrendered. And the young mistress seemed as happy over mammy's consent as she had been over her father's blessing. Mammy knew all the traditions of the section, and the histories of all the families thereabouts, and for her to set the seal of approval upon young Daniels was the final glory.

The preparations for the great wedding had gone on merrily. There was only a little time now before the auspicious day. Aunt Tempe, chief authority and owner-in-general, had been as busily engaged as any one. As the time had come nearer and nearer, though, her trouble had visibly increased, and it was the culmination of it which brought her hobbling out to chat with her master on that April evening. It must have been Maid Doshy that told her about the beautiful ceremony of giving away the bride, and described to her what a figure "Ol' Mas'" would make on the occasion, but it rankled in her mind, and she had thoughts of her own on the subject.

"Look hyeah, Mas' Stua't," she said, as she settled down on the veranda step at his feet; "I done come out hyeah to 'spute wid you."

"Well, Aunt Tempe," said Mordaunt placidly, "it won't be the first time; you've been doing that for many years. The fact is, half the time I don't know who's running this plantation, you or I. You boss the whole household round, and "the quarters" mind you better than they do the preacher. Plague take my buttons if I don't think they're afraid you'll conjure them!"

"Conju'! Who conju'! Me conju'? Wha's de mattah wid you, Mas' Stua't? You know I ain't long haided. Ef I had 'a' been, you know I'd 'a' wo'ked my roots long 'fo' now on ol' Lishy, we'en he tuk up wid dat No'ton ooman." This had happened twenty-five years before, but Stuart Mordaunt knew that it was still a sore subject with the old woman—this desertion by her husband—so he did not pursue the unpleasant matter any further.

"Well, what are you going to ' 'spute' with me about, Tempe? Ain't I running the plantation right? Or ain't your mistress behaving herself as she ought to?"

"I do wish you'd let me talk; you des' keep a-jokin' an' a runnin' on so dat a body cain't git in a wo'd aigeways."

"Well, go on."

"Now you know dat Miss 'Liza gwine ma'y?"

"Yes, she has told me about it, though I suppose she asked your consent first."

3

"Nemmine dat, nemmine dat, you hyeah me. Miss 'Liza gwine ma'y."

"Yes, unless young Daniels runs off, or sees a girl he likes better."

"Sees a gal he lak' bettah! Run off! Wha's de mattah wid you?"

The master laughed cheerily, and the old woman went on.

"Now, we all's gwineter gin huh a big weddin', des' lak my baby oughter have."

"Of course, what else do you expect? You don't suppose I'm going to have her 'jump over the broom' with him, do you?"

"Now, you listen to me: we's gwineter have all de doin's dat go 'long wid a weddin', ain't we?"

Stuart Mordaunt struck his fist on the arm of his chair and said:

"We're going to have all that the greatness of the occasion demands when a Mordaunt marries."

"Da's right, da's right. She gwineter have de o'ange wreaf an' de ring?"

"That's part of it."

"An' she gwineter be gin' erway in right style?" asked Aunt Tempe anxiously.

"To be sure."

Aunt Tempe turned her sharp black eyes on her master and shot forth her next question with sudden force and abruptness.

"Now, whut I wanter know, who gwineter gin huh erway?"

Stuart Mordaunt straightened himself up in his chair with a motion of sudden surprise and exclaimed:

"Why, Tempe, what the—what do you mean?"

"I mean des' whut I say, da's whut I mean. I wanter know who gwineter gin my Miss 'Liza erway?"

"Who should give her away?"

The old woman folded her hands calmly across her neckerchief and made answer: "Da's des' de questun."

"Why, I'm going to give my daughter away, of course."

"You gwineter gin yo' darter erway, huh, is you?" Aunt Tempe questioned slowly.

The tone was so full of contempt that her master turned a surprised look upon her face. She got up, put her hands behind her in an atti-

5

tude of defiance, and stood there looking at him, as he sat viciously biting the end of his cigar.

"You 'lows to gin huh erway, does you?"

"Why, Tempe, what the—who should give her away?"

"You 'lows to gin huh erway, I say?"

"Most assuredly I do," he answered angrily.

The old woman moved up a step higher on the porch and asked in an intense voice:

"Whut business you got givin' my chile erway? Huccome you got de right to gin Miss 'Liza to anybody?"

"Why—why—Tempe!"

"Who is you?" exclaimed Tempe. "Who raise up dat chile? Who nuss huh th'oo de colic w'en she cried all night, an' she was so peakid you didn't know w'en you gwine lay huh erway? Huh? Who do dat? Who raise you up, an' tek keer o' you, w'en yo' ol' mammy die, an' you wa'n't able even to keep erway f'om de bee-trees? Huh? Who do dat? You gin huh erway! You gin huh erway! Da's my chile, Mas' Stua't Mo'de'nt, an' ef anybody gin huh erway at de weddin', d' ain't nobody gwine do it but ol' Tempe huhself. You hyeah me?"

"But, Tempe, Tempe!" said the master, "that

6

wouldn't be proper. You can't give your young mistress away."

"P'opah er whut not, I de only one whut got de right, an' I see 'bout dat!"

Mordaunt forgot that he was talking to a servant, and sprang to his feet.

"See about it! See about it!" he cried, "I'll let you know that I can give my own daughter away when she marries. You must think you own this whole plantation, and all the white folks and niggers on it."

Aunt Tempe came up on the porch and curtsied to her master.

"Nemmine, Mas' Stua't," she said; "nemmine." Her eyes were full of tears, and her voice was trembling. "Hit all right, hit all right. I 'longs to you, but Miss 'Liza, she my chile." Her voice rose again in a defiant ring, and lost its pathos as she exclaimed, "I show you who got de right to gin my chile erway!" And shaking her turbaned head, she went back into the house mumbling to herself.

"Well!" said Stuart Mordaunt. "I'll be blessed!" He might have used a stronger term, but just then the black-coated figure of the rector came round the corner of the veranda.

"How are you, how are you, sir!" said the Rev. Mr. Davis jocosely. "Are you the man who owns this plantation?"

Mordaunt hurled his cigar down the path, and replied grimly:

"I don't know; I used to think so."

Meanwhile Aunt Tempe had gone into the house to tell her troubles to her young mistress. She and her Miss Eliza were mutually the bearers of each other's burdens on all occasions. She told her story, and laid her case before the bride-to-be.

"Now you know, baby," she said, "ef anybody got de right to gin you erway, 'tain't nobody but me."

"Yes, yes, mammy," said the young woman consolingly; "they sha'n't slight you, that they sha'n't."

"No, indeed; I don't 'tend to be slighted."

"I'll tell you what I'll do, mammy," said Miss Eliza; "even if you can't give me away, you'll be where Doshy and Dinah and none of the rest can be."

"Whah dat, chile?"

"Why, before the ceremony I'll hide you

under the portieres right back of where we're going to stand in the drawing-room."

"An' I cain't gin you erway, baby?" said the old woman sadly.

"We'll see about that, mammy; you know nobody ever knows what's going to happen."

The girl was comforting the old woman's distresses as mammy in the years gone by had quieted her childish fears. It was a putting off until to-morrow of the evils that seemed present to-day.

Aunt Tempe went away seemingly satisfied, but she thought deeply, and later she visited old Brother Parker, who used to know a servant in a preacher's family, and they talked long and earnestly together one whole evening.

Doshy saw them as they separated, and cried in derision:

"Look hyeah, Aunt Tempe, whut you an' ol' Brothah Pahkah codgin' erbout so long? 'Spec' fus' thing we knows we be gittin' slippahs an' wreafs fu you, an' you'll be follerin' Miss 'Liza's 'zample!"

"Huh-uh, chile," Aunt Tempe answered, "I ain't thinkin' nothin' 'bout may'in', case I's ol', but la, chile, I ol' in de haid, too!"

9

The preparations for the wedding were completed, and the time arrived. All the elite of the surrounding country were present. Mammy was allowed to put the last touches, insignificant though they were, to the bride's costume. She wept copiously over her child, but with not so much absorption as not to be alert when Miss Eliza took her down and slipped her behind the heavy portieres.

The organ pealed its march; the ceremony began and proceeded. The responses of the groom were strong, and those of the bride timid, but decisive and clear. Above all rose the resonant voice of the rector. Stuart Mordaunt had gathered himself together and straightened his shoulders and stepped forward at the words, "Who giveth this woman," when suddenly the portieres behind the bridal party were thrown asunder, and the ample form of Aunt Tempe appeared. The whole assemblage was thunderstruck. The minister paused, Mordaunt stood transfixed; a hush fell upon all of them, which was broken by the old woman's stentorian voice crying:

"I does! Dat's who! I gins my baby erway!"

For an instant no one spoke; some of the older

ladies wiped tears from their eyes, and Stuart
Mordaunt bowed and resumed his place beside
his daughter. The clergyman took up the ceremony where he had left off, and the marriage
was finished without any further interruption.

When it was all over, neither the father, the
mother, the proud groom, nor the blushing bride
had one word of reproach for mammy, for no
one doubted that her giving away and her blessing were as effectual and fervent as those of the
nearest relative could have been.

And Aunt Tempe chuckled as she went her
way. "I showed 'em. I showed 'em."

AUNT TEMPE'S REVENGE.

Laramie Belle—why she was Laramie Belle
no one could ever make out—Laramie Belle had
astonished the whole plantation. She came of
stock that was prone to perpetrating surprises,
and she did credit to her blood and breeding.
When she was only two weeks old the wiseacres
had said that no good could ever come to so out-
rageously a named child. Aunt Mandy had
quite expressed the opinion of every one, when
she said: "Why, ef de chile had been named a
puoh Bible name er a puoh devil name, she
mought a' mounted to somep'n', but dat aih con-
traption, Laramie Belle, ain't one ner 'tothah.
She done doomed a'ready." And here was Laramie Belle after eighteen years of a rather quiet
life, getting ready to fulfill all the adverse
prophecies.

There were, perhaps, two elements in the matter that made the Mordaunt plantation look
upon it with less leniency even than usual. Of
course, it was the unwritten law of the little community that alliances should not be contracted

with people off the estate. But even they knew that love must go where it will, and a certain latitude might have been allowed the culprit had she not been guilty of another heresy that made her crime blacker. Incredible as it may seem, at the very time that Tom Norton began bestowing his impudent attentions upon her, Julius, the coachman, had also deigned to look at her with favor. For her to give the preference to the former was an offence not to be overlooked nor condoned. By so doing, she not only lost a golden matrimonial opportunity, but belittled the value of her own people.

There was another feeling that entered into the trouble, too, a vague, almost shadowy dislike to the man upon whom Laramie Belle had placed her affections. Although only a tradition to the younger servants, the memory was still vivid in the minds of the older heads of Aunt Tempe's desertion by her husband, when he took up with "the Norton woman." They remembered how Tempe, then a spirited, lively woman, had mourned and refused to be comforted, and they could not forget the bravery with which she had consented that Stuart Mordaunt should transfer her husband to Master Norton, in order that he might be with his new wife. She had mourned for weeks, yes, for months, and no one else had ever come into her heart. Was it not enough that this suffering had come to a Mordaunt through this Norton wench, without this man, this son of her and her stolen mate, taking away one of the plantation's buds of promise?

They talked much to Laramie Belle, but she was not a girl of many words, and only held her head down and made imaginary lines with her foot as she listened. She would not talk to them about it, but neither would she give up Tom and encourage Julius.

There were those who believed that she was encouraged in her stubborness by her mother, that mother who had closed her ears to all advice, remonstrance, and prophecy when warned as to the naming of her baby. They were right, too, for Lucy did uphold her daughter's quiet independence. Indeed, there was a streak of strangeness in both of them that, in spite of the younger woman's popularity, placed them, as it were, in a position apart.

"You right, honey," said her mother to her, "ef you loves Tom No'ton you tek up wid him; don' keer whut de res' says. Yo' got to live wid

him, yo' got to do his cookin' an' washin' an'
i'nin', an' all you got to do is to git Mas' Stua't
to say yes to you."

No one argued with Lucy, whatever they
might say to her daughter. About the older
woman there was a spirit fierce and free that
would not be gainsaid. There was something of
the wild nerve of African forests about her that
had not yet been driven out by the hard hand of
slavery, nor yet smoothed down by the velvet
glove of irresponsibility. The essence of this,
albeit subdued, refined, diluted, perhaps, was in
her daughter, and that was why she kept her way
in spite of all opposition.

As for Tom Norton, opposition only made
him more determined, and nothing did him more
good than to laugh in the face of Julius as he
was leaving the Mordaunt place after a pleasant
visit with Laramie.

As promiscuous visiting between the plantations was forbidden, Tom had had the good
sense to secure both his master's and Stuart Mordaunt's consent, the latter's reluctantly given to
these excursions. On the principle, however, that
he who is given much may with safety take more,
he often overstepped the bound and went to see

his sweetheart when the permission was wanting. Julius found this out and determined to administer a severe lesson to his rival on the first occasion that he found him within his domain without his master's permission. So thinking, he laid his plans carefully, the first of them being to gain a friend and informant on the Norton place. This he succeeded in doing, and then, after confiding in a couple of trusted friends, he lay in wait for his unfortunate rival. He had a stout hickory stick in his hand, and he and his friends were stationed at short intervals of space along the road which Tom must cross to visit Laramie Belle.

It was a moonlit night. The watchers by the roadside heard the sound of his footsteps as their victim approached. But, with ghoulish satisfaction, they let him pass on. It was not now that they wanted him, but when he came back. Then they would have the fun of whipping him to his very gate, and he would not dare to tell. They possessed their souls in patience, and waited, chuckling ever and anon at the prospect as the first hour passed. They yawned more and chuckled less through the second hour. During the third, the yawns held exclusive sway. He

was staying particularly late that night. It was
in the gray dawn that, unsatisfied, sleepy, and
angry, they took their way home. Their heads
seemed scarcely to have touched the pillows when
the horns and bells sounded the rising hour. Oh,
misery! They had missed Tom, too.

Julius could not understand it. It was very
simple, though. Man proposes, but woman ex-
poses, and he had not learned to beware of a
friend who had a wife. So, his secret had leaked
out. Laramie Belle had had a chance to warn
Tom, and, going by another road, he had been
in bed and snoring when his watchers were wear-
ily waiting for him by the roadside.

Even for the coachman's friends, the story was
too good to keep, and before long big house and
quarters were laughing to their hearts' content.

The unwelcome suitor was doubly unfortunate, however, for his action precipitated the
result which he was so anxious to prevent. Seeing himself in danger of being the constant victim of intrigue and molestation, Tom Norton
determined to press his suit and bring matters to
a close. With this end in view he sought his
master and laid the case before him, begging for
his intercession. Norton, the master, promised

to visit Stuart Mordaunt and talk the matter over with him.

He did so. He laid the case before Mordaunt plainly and clearly. A negro on his plantation was in love with one of his host's maids. What was to be done about it?

"Well, it's this way, Norton," said Mordaunt frankly. "You know I never have countenanced this mating of servants off the plantation. It's only happened once, and you know how that was."

"I know, but, Mr. Mordaunt, Tom likes that wench, and if he don't get her it'll make a bad darky out of him, that's all; and he'll be a trouble to your plantation as well as to mine."

"Oh, I can answer as to mine."

"Perhaps, but there's no telling what influence he might have over your people, and that's worth looking into."

"You're on the wrong road to accomplish your end with me, Norton."

"But you don't understand; I'm not talking for myself, but for the happiness of a boy that I like."

"You know how I handled a similar case."

"Yes; but I'm a poorer man than you, and I—well, I can't afford to be generous."

Mordaunt laughed coldly. "Well," he said, "I don't like the stock of that boy Tom. You know how his father treated Tempe, and—oh, well, Norton, see me again, I'm not in the mood to discuss this matter now," and he rose to dismiss his visitor.

"I'll sell Tom cheap," said Norton.

"In spite of your deep feeling for him?"

"My deep feeling for him prompts me to help him to happiness."

"Very considerate of you, Norton, but I'm not buying or selling darkies. Good-day."

Norton ground his teeth as he walked away. "That proud fool despises me," he murmured angrily, "but either he shall buy Tom or that nigger shall make him more than his money's worth of trouble."

Stuart Mordaunt went away from the interview with his neighbor with a sneer on his lips. He despised Aldberry Norton, not because he was a poorer man, but because he was a man with no principle. Once an overseer, now a small owner, he brought the manners of the lower position to the higher one.

"I'd buy Tom," he said to himself, "just to satisfy Laramie Belle, if it wasn't against my principle."

When the plantation, through some mysterious intelligence, heard how Tom's suit fared, it was exultant. After all, the flower of their girls was not to go away to mate with an inferior. They ceased to laugh at Julius behind his back. But there is no accounting for the ways of women, and at this time Laramie Belle ceased speaking to him—so, setting one off against the other, the poor coachman had little to pride himself upon.

The girl now had fewer words than ever. Her smiles, too, were fewer, and she was often in tears. Seeing her thus, the fierceness in her mother's face and manner increased until it grew to be a settled fact that one who cared for his life was not to bother Laramie Belle nor Lucy.

During all the trouble, Aunt Tempe had listened and looked on, unmoved. Every one had expected her to take a very decided part against the welcome suitor, the son of her old rival and her defaulting husband; but she had not done so. She had stood aloof until this crisis came. Even now, she was strangely subdued. Only she cast inquiring glances at Laramie Belle's long, tear-saddened face whenever she passed her. Day by day she saw how the girl faded, and then came the wrath of the plantation upon her. When they saw that she would not yield, they cast her off. They would not associate with her, nor speak to her. She was none of theirs. Let her find her friends over at Norton's, they said. They laughed at her and tossed their heads in her face, and she went her way silent but weeping. Lucy's eyes grew fierce. Something strange, foreign, even wild within her seemed to rear itself and call for release. But she held herself as if saying, "A little while yet."

The day came, however, when Aunt Tempe could stand Laramie Belle's sad face no longer. It may have been the influence of Parker's words as he told of the command to do good to "dem dat spitefully use you," or it may have been the strong promptings of her own good heart that drove Tempe to seek her master out.

"Well, Tempe," said Mordaunt, as he saw that she had settled herself for a talk with him, "what now?"

"It's des' anothah one o' my 'sputes," said

Tempe, with an embarrassment entirely new to her.

"Well, what's coming now?"

"Mas' Stua't, I's an' ol' fool, dat's what I is."

"Ah, Tempe, have you found that out? Then you begin to be wise. It's wonderful how as you and I get old we both arrive at the same conclusions."

"I aint jokin', Mas' Stua't. I's mighty anxious. I been thinkin' 'bout Tawm an' La'-amie Belle."

"Now, Tempe!"

"Hol' on, Mas'. Yo' know de reason I got some right to think 'bout dem two. Mas' Stua't, my ol' man didn' do me right to leave me an' tek up wid anothah 'ooman."

"He was a hound."

"Look-a-hyeah, whut you talkin' 'bout? You heish. I was a gwine 'long to say dat my man didn' treat me right, but sence it's done, it's done, an' de only way to do is to mek de bes' of it."

"You've been doing that for a good many years."

"Yes, but it wasn't wid my willin' hea't. Brothah Pahkah say 'dough dat we mus' do good to dem what spitefully use us."

22

"What are you driving at, Tempe?"

"Mas' Stua't, sence Tawm No'ton, he my ol' man's boy, don't you reckon I's some kin' of a step-mammy to him?"

Stuart Mordaunt could not repress a chuckle as he answered, "Well, I can't just figure out any such kinship."

"I don' keer whut yo' figgers out. Hit's got to be so 'cause I feels it."

"It must be so, then."

"Well, de plantation done cas' La'amie Belle out 'cause she love Tawm, an' she cryin' huh eyes out. Tawm, he feel moughty bad 'bout it."

"Well?"

"Mas' Stua't, let 'em ma'y."

"Tempe, you know I object to the servants marrying off the plantation."

"I know, but—"

"And you know that I can't buy Tom."

"Won't you, des' dis time?"

"No, I won't; I'm not a nigger trader, and I won't have any one making me one. You let me alone, Tempe, and don't concern yourself in this business."

"Dey des two po' chillen, Mas' Stua't."

"I don't care if they are. I won't have anything to do with it, I tell you. I won't have my people marrying with Norton's, and if he can't make a fair exchange for the man I gave him, why, Tom and Laramie Belle will have to give each other up, that's all."

Aunt Tempe said no more, but went tearfully away, but out of the corner of her eye she saw her master pacing up and down long after she had left him, and she had the satisfaction of knowing he was uneasy.

"Confound Tempe," Mordaunt was saying. "Why can't she let me alone? Just as I quiet my conscience, here she comes and knocks everything into a cocked hat. I won't buy Tom. I won't, that's all there is about it. Her stepson, indeed!" He tried to laugh, but it ended lamely. "Confound Tempe," he repeated.

He was troubled for two or three days, and then with a very sheepish expression he went to Tempe's cabin.

"Tempe," he said, "you've served me long and faithfully, and I've been thinking about making you a present for some time."

"La, Mas' Stua't, wha's de mattah wid you?"

"You hush up. Here's some money, you can

do with it as you please," and he thrust a roll of bills into her hand.

"W'y, Mas' Stua't Mo'da'nt, is you clean loony? What is I gwine to do wid all dis money?"

"Throw it in the fire, confound you, if you haven't got sense enough to know what use to put it to!" Stuart Mordaunt shouted, as he turned away. Then the light dawned on Aunt Tempe, and she sank to her knees with a prayer of thanks.

It took but a short time for her to have a less scrupulous man buy Tom for her, and then with a solemnity as great as his own, she presented him to her master, who received him, as he said, in the spirit in which he was given.

Lucy and Laramie Belle were present at the ceremony. The fierce light had died out of Lucy's eyes, and Laramie's face was aglow. When it was all over, Julius shook hands with Tom as an acknowledgment of defeat, and that gave the cue to the rest of the plantation, who forgot at once all its animosities against the new fellow-servant. But there were some things which the author of all this good could not forget, and on the night of the wedding, when the others rejoiced, Aunt Tempe wept and murmured: "He might 'a' been mine, he might 'a' been mine."

THE WALLS OF JERICHO.

Parker was sitting alone under the shade of a locust tree at the edge of a field. His head was bent and he was deep in thought. Every now and then there floated to him the sound of vociferous singing, and occasionally above the music rose the cry of some shouting brother or sister. But he remained in his attitude of meditation as if the singing and the cries meant nothing to him.

They did, however, mean much, and, despite his outward impassiveness, his heart was in a tumult of wounded pride and resentment. He had always been so faithful to his flock, constant in attendance and careful of their welfare. Now it was very hard, at the first call of the stranger to have them leave their old pastor and crowd to the new exhorter.

It was nearly a week before that a free negro had got permission to hold meetings in the wood adjoining the Mordaunt estate. He had invited the negroes of the surrounding plantations to come and bring their baskets with them that they might serve the body while they saved the soul. By ones and twos Parker had seen his congregation drop away from him until now, in the cabin meeting house where he held forth, only a few retainers, such as Mandy and Dinah and some of the older ones on the plantation, were present to hear him. It grieved his heart, for he had been with his flock in sickness and in distress, in sorrow and in trouble, but now, at the first approach of the rival they could and did desert him. He felt it the more keenly because he knew just how powerful this man Johnson was. He was loud-voiced and theatrical, and the fact that he invited all to bring their baskets gave his scheme added influence; for his congregations flocked to the meetings as to a holy picnic. It was seldom that they were thus able to satisfy both the spiritual and material longings at the same time.

Parker had gone once to the meeting and had hung unobserved on the edge of the crowd; then he saw by what power the preacher held the people. Every night, at the very height of the service, he would command the baskets to be opened and the people, following the example of the children of Israel, to march, munching their food, round and round the inclosure, as their Biblical archetypes had marched around the walls of Jericho. Parker looked on and smiled grimly. He knew, and the sensational revivalist knew, that there were no walls there to tumble down, and that the spiritual significance of the performance was entirely lost upon the people. Whatever may be said of the Mordaunt plantation exhorter, he was at least no hypocrite, and he saw clearly that his rival gave to the emotional negroes a breathing chance and opportunity to eat and a way to indulge their dancing proclivities by marching trippingly to a spirited tune.

He went away in disgust and anger, but thoughts deeper than either burned within him. He was thinking some such thoughts now as he sat there on the edge of the field listening to the noise of the basket meeting. It was unfortunate for his peace of mind that while he sat there absorbed in resentful musings two of the young men of his master's household should come along. They did not know how Parker felt about the matter, or they never would have allowed themselves to tease him on the score of his people's defection.

"Well, Parker," said Ralph, "seems mighty strange to me that you are not down there in the woods at the meeting."

The old man was silent.

"I am rather surprised at Parker myself," said Tom Mordaunt; "knowing how he enjoys a good sermon I expected him to be over there. They do say that man Johnson is a mighty preacher."

Still Parker was silent.

"Most of your congregation are over there," Ralph resumed. Then the old exhorter, stung into reply, raised his head and said quietly:

"Dat ain't nuffin' strange, Mas' Ralph. I been preachin' de gospel on yo' father's plantation, night aftah night, nigh on to twenty-five years, an' spite o' dat, mos' o' my congregation is in hell."

"That doesn't speak very well for your preaching," said Ralph, and the two young fellows laughed heartily.

"Come, Parker, come, don't be jealous; come on over to the meeting with us, and let us see what it is that Johnson has that you haven't. You know any man can get a congregation about him, but it takes some particular power to hold them after they are caught."

Parker rose slowly from the ground and reluctantly joined his two young masters as they made their way toward the woods. The service was in full swing. At a long black log, far to the front, there knelt a line of mourners wailing and praying, while the preacher stood above them waving his hands and calling on them to believe and be saved. Every now and then some one voluntarily broke into a song, either a stirring, marching spiritual or some soft crooning melody that took strange hold upon the hearts of even the most skeptical listeners. As they approached and joined the crowd some one had just swung into the undulating lilt of

> "Some one buried in de graveyard,
>   Some one buried in de sea, .
> All come togethah in de mo'nin',
>   Go soun' de Jubilee."

Just the word "Jubilee" was enough to start the whole throng into agitated life, and they moaned and shouted and wailed until the forest became a pandemonium.

Johnson, the preacher, saw Parker approach with the two young men and a sudden spirit of conquest took possession of him. He felt that he owed it to himself to crystallize his triumph over the elder exhorter. So, with a glance that begged for approbation, he called aloud:

"Open de baskets! Rise up, fu' de Jericho

walls o' sin is a-stan'in'. You 'member dey ma'ched roun' seven times, an' at de sevent' time de walls a-begun to shake an' shiver; de foundations a-begun to trimble; de chillen a-hyeahed de rum'lin' lak a thundah f'om on high, an' putty soon down come de walls a-fallin' an' a-crum'lin'! Oh, brothahs an' sistahs, let us a-ma'ch erroun' de walls o' Jericho to-night seven times, an' a-eatin' o' de food dat de Lawd has pervided us wid. Dey ain't no walls o' brick an' stone a-stan'in' hyeah to-night, but by de eye o' Christian faif I see a great big wall o' sin a-stan'in' strong an' thick hyeah in ouah midst. Is we gwine to let it stan'?"

"Oh, no, no!" moaned the people.

"Is we gwine to ma'ch erroun' dat wall de same ez Joshuay an' his ban' did in de days of ol', ontwell we hyeah de cracklin' an' de rum'lin', de breakin' an' de taihin', de onsettlin' of de foundations an' de fallin' of de stones an' mo'tah?" Then raising his voice he broke into the song:

"Den we'll ma'ch, ma'ch down, ma'ch, ma'ch
        down,
    Oh, chillen, ma'ch down,
    In de day o' Jubilee."

The congregation joined him in the ringing chorus, and springing to their feet began marching around and around the inclosure, chewing vigorously in the breathing spaces of the hymn.

The two young men, who were too used to such sights to be provoked to laughter, nudged each other and bent their looks upon Parker, who stood with bowed head, refusing to join in the performance, and sighed audibly.

After the march Tom and Ralph started for home, and Parker went with them.

"He's very effective, don't you think so, Tom?" said Ralph.

"Immensely so," was the reply. "I don't know that I have ever seen such a moving spectacle."

"The people seem greatly taken up with him."

"Personal magnetism, that's what it is. Don't you think so, Parker?"

"Hum," said Parker.

"It's a wonderful idea of his, that marching around the walls of sin."

"So original, too. It's a wonder you never thought of a thing like that, Parker. I believe it would have held your people to you in the face of everything. They do love to eat and march."

"Well," said Parker, "you all may think what you please, but I ain't nevah made no business of mekin' a play show outen de Bible. Dem folks don't know what dey're doin'. Why, ef dem niggahs hyeahed anything commence to fall they'd taih dat place up gittin' erway f'om daih. It's a wondah de Lawd don' sen' a jedgmen' on 'em fu' tu'nin' His wo'd into mockery."

The two young men bit their lips and a knowing glance flashed between them. The same idea had leaped into both of their minds at once. They said no word to Parker, however, save at parting, and then they only begged that he would go again the next night of the meeting.

"You must, Parker," said Ralph. "You must represent the spiritual interest of the plantation. If you don't, that man Johnson will think we are heathen or that our exhorter is afraid of him."

At the name of fear the old preacher bridled and said with angry dignity:

"Nemmine, nemmine; he shan't nevah think dat. I'll be daih."

Parker went alone to his cabin, sore at heart; the young men, a little regretful that they had stung him a bit too far, went up to the big house, their heads close together, and in the darkness and stillness there came to them the hymns of the people.

On the next night Parker went early to the meeting-place and, braced by the spirit of his defiance, took a conspicuous front seat. His face gave no sign, though his heart throbbed angrily as he saw the best and most trusted of his flock come in with intent faces and seat themselves anxiously to await the advent of an alien. Why had those rascally boys compelled him for his own dignity's sake to come there? Why had they forced him to be a living witness of his own degradation and of his own people's ingratitude?

But Parker was a diplomat, and when the hymns began he joined his voice with the voices of the rest.

Something, though, tugged at Parker's breast, a vague hoped-for something; he knew not what —the promise of relief from the tension of his jealousy, the harbinger of revenge. It was in the air. Everything was tense as if awaiting the moment of catastrophe. He found himself joyous, and when Johnson arose on the wings of his eloquence it was Parker's loud "Amen" which set fire to all the throng. Then, when the meeting was going well, when the spiritual fire had been thoroughly kindled and had gone from crackling to roaring; when the hymns were loudest and the hand-clapping strongest, the revivalist called upon them to rise and march around the walls of Jericho. Parker rose with the rest, and, though he had no basket, he levied on the store of a solicitous sister and marched with them, singing, singing, but waiting, waiting for he knew not what.

It was the fifth time around and yet nothing had happened. Then the sixth, and a rumbling sound was heard near at hand. A tree crashed down on one side. White eyes were rolled in the direction of the noise and the burden of the hymn was left to the few faithful. Half way around and the bellow of a horn broke upon the startled people's ears, and the hymn sank lower and lower. The preacher's face was ashen, but he attempted to inspire the people, until on the seventh turn such a rumbling and such a clattering, such a tumbling of rocks, such a falling of trees as was never heard before gave horror to the night. The people paused for one moment and then the remains of the bread and meat were cast to the winds, baskets were thrown away, and

" ' STAN' STILL, STAN' STILL—AN' SEE DE SALVATION ' "

the congregation, thoroughly maddened with fear, made one rush for the road and the quarters. Ahead of them all, his long coat-tails flying and his legs making not steps but leaps, was the Rev. Mr. Johnson. He had no word of courage or hope to offer the frightened flock behind him. Only Parker, with some perception of the situation, stood his ground. He had leaped upon a log and was crying aloud:

"Stan' still, stan' still, I say, an' see de salvation," but he got only frightened, backward glances as the place was cleared.

When they were all gone, he got down off the log and went to where several of the trees had fallen. He saw that they had been cut nearly through during the day on the side away from the clearing, and ropes were still along the upper parts of their trunks. Then he chuckled softly to himself. As he stood there in the dim light of the fat-pine torches that were burning themselves out, two stealthy figures made their way out of the surrounding gloom into the open space. Tom and Ralph were holding their sides, and Parker, with a hand on the shoulder of each of the boys, laughed unrighteously.

"Well, he hyeahed de rum'lin' an' crum'lin'," he said, and Ralph gasped.

"You're the only one who stood your ground, Parker," said Tom.

"How erbout de walls o' Jericho now?" was all Parker could say as he doubled up.

When the people came back to their senses they began to realize that the Rev. Mr. Johnson had not the qualities of a leader. Then they recalled how Parker had stood still in spite of the noise and called them to wait and see the salvation, and so, with a rush of emotional feeling, they went back to their old allegiance. Parker's meeting-house again was filled, and for lack of worshipers Mr. Johnson held no more meetings and marched no more around the walls of Jericho.

HOW BROTHER PARKER FELL FROM GRACE.

It all happened so long ago that it has almost been forgotten upon the plantation, and few save the older heads know anything about it save from hearsay. It was in Parker's younger days, but the tale was told on him for a long time, until he was so old that every little disparagement cut him like a knife. Then the young scapegraces who had the story only from their mothers' lips spared his dotage. Even to young eyes, the respect which hedges about the form of eighty obscures many of the imperfections that are apparent at twenty-eight, and Parker was nearing eighty.

The truth of it is that Parker, armed with the authority which his master thought the due of the plantation exhorter, was wont to use his power with rather too free a rein. He was so earnest for the spiritual welfare of his fellow-servants that his watchful ministrations became a nuisance and a bore.

Even Aunt Doshy, who was famous for her devotion to all that pertained to the church, had been heard to state that "Brothah Pahkah was a moughty powahful 'zortah, but he sholy was monst'ous biggity." This from a member of his flock old enough to be his mother, quite summed up the plantation's estimate of this black disciple.

There was many a time when it would have gone hard with Brother Parker among the young bucks on the Mordaunt plantation but that there was scarcely one of them but could remember a time when Parker had come to his cabin to console some sick one, help a seeker, comfort the dying or close the eyes of one already dead, and it clothed him about with a sacredness, which, however much inclined, they dared not invade.

"Ain't it enough," Mandy's Jim used to say, "fu' Brothah Pahkah to 'tend to his business down at meetin' widout spookin' 'roun' all de cabins an' outhouses? Seems to me dey's enough dev'ment gwine on right undah his nose widout him gwine 'roun' tryin' to smell out what's hid."

Every secret sinner on the place agreed with this dictum, and it came to the preacher's ears. He smiled broadly.

"Uh, huh," he remarked, "hit's de stuck pig dat squeals. I reckon Jim's up to some'p'n right

now, an' I lay I'll fin' out what dat some'p'n is."
Parker was a subtle philosopher and Jim had
by his remark unwittingly disclosed his interest
in the preacher's doings. It then behooved his
zealous disciple to find out the source of this un-
usual interest and opposition.

On the Sunday following his sermon was
strong, fiery and convincing. His congregation
gave themselves up to the joy of the occasion and
lost all consciousness of time or place in their
emotional ecstacy. But, although he continued
to move them with his eloquence, not for one moment did Parker lose possession of himself. His
eyes roamed over the people before him and took
in the absence of several who had most loudly
and heartily agreed with Jim's dictum. Jim himself was not there.

"Uh, huh," said the minister to himself even
in the midst of his exhortations. "Uh, huh, erway on some dev'ment, I be boun'." He could
hardly wait to hurry through his sermon. Then
he seized his hat and almost ran away from the
little table that did duty as a pulpit desk. He
brushed aside with scant ceremony those who
would have asked him to their cabins to share
some special delicacy, and made his way swiftly

to the door. There he paused and cast a wondering glance about the plantation.

"I des wondah whaih dem scoun'els is mos' lakly to be." Then his eye fell upon an old half-ruined smoke-house that stood between the kitchen and the negro quarters, and he murmured to himself, "Lak ez not, lak ez not." But he did not start directly for the object of his suspicions. Oh, no, he was too deep a diplomat for that. He knew that if there were wrongdoers in that inno-cent-looking ruin they would be watching in his direction about the time when they expected meeting to be out; so he walked off swiftly, but carelessly, in an opposite direction, and, instead of going straight past the kitchen, began to cir-cle around from the direction of the quarters, whence no danger would be apprehended.

As he drew nearer and nearer the place, he thought he heard the rise and fall of eager voices. He approached more cautiously. Now he was perfectly sure that he could hear smothered con-versation, and he smiled grimly as he pictured to himself the surprise of his quarry when he should come up with them. He was almost upon the smoke-house now. Those within were so absorbed that the preacher was able to creep up and peer through a crack at the scene within.

There, seated upon the earthen floor, were the unregenerate of the plantation. In the very midst of them was Mandy's Jim, and he was dealing from a pack of greasy cards.

It is a wonder that they did not hear the preacher's gasp of horror as he stood there gazing upon the iniquitous performance. But they did not. The delight of High-Low-Jack was too absorbing for that, and they suspected nothing of Parker's presence until he slipped around to the door, pushed it open and confronted them like an accusing angel.

Jim leaped to his feet with a strong word upon his lips.

"I reckon you done fu'got, Brothah Jim, what day dis is," said the preacher.

"I ain't fu'got nuffin," was the dogged reply; "I don't see what you doin' roun' hyeah nohow."

"I's a lookin' aftah some strayin' lambs," said Parker, "an' I done foun' 'em. You ought to be ashamed o' yo'se'ves, evah one o' you, playin' cyards on de Lawd's day."

There was the light of reckless deviltry in Jim's eyes.

"Dey ain't no h'am in a little game o' cyards."

"Co'se not, co'se not," replied the preacher scornfully. "Dem's des de sins that's ca'ied many a man to hell wid his eyes wide open, de little no-ha'm kin'."

"I don't reckon you evah played cyards," said Jim sneeringly.

"Yes, I has played, an' I thought I was enjoyin' myse'f ontwell I foun' out dat it was all wickedness an' idleness."

"Oh, I don't reckon you was evah ve'y much of a player. I know lots o' men who has got u'ligion des case dey couldn't win at cyards."

The company greeted this sally with a laugh and then looked aghast at Jim's audacity.

"U'ligion's a moughty savin' to de pocket," Jim went on. "We kin believe what we wants to, and I say you nevah was no playah, an' dat's de reason you tuk up de Gospel."

"Hit ain't so. I 'low dey was a time when I could 'a' outplayed any one o' you sinnahs hyeah, but——"

"Prove it!" The challenge shot forth like a pistol's report.

Parker hesitated. "What you mean?" he said.

How Brother Parker Fell from Grace

"Beat me, beat all of us, an' we'll believe you didn't quit playin' case you allus lost. You a preachah now, an' I daih you."

Parker's face turned ashen and his hands gripped together. He was young then, and the hot blood sped tumultuously through his veins.

"Prove it," said Jim; "you cain't. We'd play you outen yo' coat an' back into de pulpit ag'in."

"You would, would you?" The light of battle was in Parker's eyes, the desire for conquest throbbing in his heart. "Look a'hyeah, Jim, Sunday er no Sunday, preachah er no preachah, I play you th'ee games fu' de Gospel's sake." And the preacher sat down in the circle, his face tense with anger at his tormentor's insinuations. He did not see the others around him. He saw only Jim, the man who had spoken against his cloth. He did not see the look of awe and surprise upon the faces of the others, nor did he note that one of the assembly slipped out of the shed just as the game began.

Jim found the preacher no mean antagonist, but it mattered little to him whether he won or not. His triumph was complete when he succeeded in getting this man, who kept the conscience of the plantation, to sin as others sinned.

45

"I see you ain't fu'got yo' cunnin'," he remarked as the preacher dealt in turn.

"'Tain't no time to talk now," said Parker fiercely.

The excitement of the onlookers grew more and more intense. They were six and six, and it was the preacher's deal. His eyes were bright, and he was breathing quickly. Parker was a born fighter and nothing gave him more joy than the heat of the battle itself. He riffled the cards. Jim cut. He dealt and turned Jack. Jim laughed.

"You know the trick," he said.

"Dat's one game," said Parker, and bent over the cards as they came to him. He did not hear a light step outside nor did he see a shadow that fell across the open doorway. He was just about to lead when a cold voice, full of contempt, broke upon his ear and made him keep the card he would have played poised in his hand.

"And so these are your after-meeting diversions, are they, Parker?" said his master's voice.

Stuart Mordaunt was standing in the door, his face cold and stern, while his informant grinned maliciously.

"HIS EYES WERE BRIGHT, AND HE WAS BREATHING
QUICKLY"

Parker brushed his hand across his brow as if dazed.

"Well, Mas' Stua't, he do play monst'ous well fu' a preachah," said his tempter.

The preacher at these words looked steadily at Jim, and then the realization of his position burst upon him. The tiger in him came uppermost and, with flaming eyes, he took a quick step toward Jim.

"Stop," said Mordaunt, coming between them; don't add anything more to what you have already done."

"Mas' Stua't, I—I——" Parker broke down, and, turning away from the exultant faces, rushed headlong out of the place. His master followed more leisurely, angry and hurt at the hypocrisy of a trusted servant.

Of course the game was over for that day, but Jim and his companions hung around the smoke-house for some time, rejoicing in the downfall of their enemy. Afterward, they went to their cabins for dinner. Then Jim made a mistake. With much laughter and boasting he told Mandy all about it, and then suddenly awakened to the fact that she was listening to him with a face on which only horror was written. Jim turned to his meal in silence and disgust. A woman has no sense of humor.

"Whaih you gwine?" he asked, as Mandy began putting on her bonnet and shawl with ominous precision.

"I's gwine up to de big house, dat's whaih I's gwine."

"What you gwine daih fu'?"

"I's gwine to tell Mas' Stua't all erbout hit."

"Don't you daih."

"Heish yo' mouf. Don't you talk to me, you nasty, low-life scamp. I's gwine tell Mas' Stua't, an' I hope an' pray he'll tek all de hide offen yo back."

Jim sat in bewildered misery as Mandy flirted out of the cabin; he felt vaguely some of the hopelessness of defeat which comes to a man whenever he attempts to lay sacrilegious hands on a woman's religion or what stands to her for religion.

Parker was sitting alone in his cabin with bowed head when the door opened and his master came across the floor and laid his hand gently on the negro's shoulder.

"I didn't know how it was, Parker." he said softly.

How Brother Parker Fell from Grace

"Oh, I's back-slid, I's fell from grace," moaned Parker.

"Nonsense," said his master, "you've fallen from nothing. There are times when we've got to meet the devil on his own ground and fight him with his own weapons."

Parker raised his head gladly. "Say dem wo'ds ag'in, Mas' Stua't," he said.

His master repeated the words, but added: "But it isn't safe to go into the devil's camp too often, Parker."

"I ain't gwine into his camp no mo'. Aftah dis I's gwine to stan' outside an' hollah in." His face was beaming and his voice trembled with joy.

"I didn't think I'd preach to-night," he said timidly.

"Of course you will," said Mordaunt, "and your mistress and I are coming to hear you, so do your best."

His master went out and Parker went down on his knees.

He did preach that night and the plantation remembered the sermon.

THE TROUSERS.

It was a nasty, rainy Sunday morning. The dripping skies lowered forbiddingly and the ground about the quarters was slippery with mud and punctuated with frequent dirty puddles where the rain had collected in the low spots. Through this Brother Parker, like the good pastor that he was, was carefully picking his way toward the log meeting house on the border of the big woods, for neither storm nor rain could keep him away from his duty however careless his flock might prove. He was well on his way when he was arrested by the sound of a voice calling him from one of the cabins, and Ike, one of the hands, came running after him. His wife, Caroline, was sick, and as she could not get to church, she desired the pastor's immediate spiritual ministrations at her own house.

The preacher turned back eagerly. His duty was always sweet to him and nothing gave him so keen a sense of pleasure as to feel that he was hurried to attend to all that needed him—that one duty crowded upon the heels of another. Moreover, he was a strong man of prayer in the sick room and some word that he should say might fall as a seed upon the uncultivated ground of Ike's heart, or if not, that he might heap coals of fire upon his head, for he was still a sinner.

With these thoughts and speculations in his mind, he started back to the cabin. But alas, for his haste, a sneaking, insidious piece of land lay in wait for him. Upon this he stepped. In another instant, his feet were pointing straight before him and he sat down suddenly in one of the biggest of the mud puddles. The tails of his long coat spread out about him and covered him like a blanket.

"Oomph!" he exclaimed as if the impact had driven the word from his lips, and for a moment he sat looking pitifully up into Ike's face, as if to see if there were any laughter there. But there was no mirth in the younger man's countenance.

"Did you hu't yo'se'f, Brother Pahkah?" he asked, offering his hand.

"Well, seems like hit's shuck me up a leetle. But I reckon hit'll des' settle my bones mo' natchally fu' de grave."

"Hit's too bad I had to call you. Hit nevah would a' happened if it hadn't a been fu' dat."

"Heish, man. Hit's all right. De shephud

muss answeh de call o' de lambs, don' keer whut
de weathah an' whut de tribbilations, dat's what
he fu'."

The old man spoke heroically, but he felt rue-
fully his soaking and damaged trousers even
while the words were on his lips.

"Well, let's pu'su' ouah way."

He took up his hurried walk again and led Ike
to his own door, the cloth of his garments stick-
ing to him and the tails of his coat flapping damp-
ly about his legs.

It has been maintained, with some degree of
authority to enforce the statement, that the
Americanized African is distinctly averse to cold
water. If this is true, Parker was giving a glowing illustration of the warmth of his religion or
the strength of his endurance, for not once did
he murmur or make mention of his wet clothes
even when the sick woman, all unconscious of his
misfortune, started in upon a long history of her
bodily ailments and spiritual experiences. He
gave her sound pastoral advice, condoled with
her and prayed with her. But when his ministrations were over, something like a sigh of relief
broke from the old man's breast.

He turned at once to Ike: "Brothah Ike," he

said. "I's feared to go on to meetin' in dese pants. I's ol' an' dey ain't no tellin' but I'd tek col'. Has you got a spaih paih 'bout?"

Ike was suddenly recalled to himself, and his wife, upon hearing the matter explained, was for getting up and helping to brush and fix up the none too neat pair of trousers that her husband found for the preacher. Dissuaded from doing this, she was loud in denunciations of her innocent self for keeping brother Parker so long in his wet garments. But the old man, thankful to get out of them at last, bade her not to worry.

"I reckon it's de oldes' hosses aftah all dat kin stan' de ha'des' whacks," he said, and with these cheery words hastened off to meeting.

As was to be expected, he was late in arriving, and his congregation were singing hymn after hymn as he came up in order to pass the time and keep themselves in the spirit. It warmed his heart as he heard the rolling notes and he was all ready to dash into his sermon as soon as he was seated before the table that did duty as a reading desk. He flung himself into the hymn with all the power that was in him, and even before his opening prayer was done, the congregation showed that it was unable to contain its holy joy.

"Ol' Brothah Pahkah sholy is full of de spirit dis mo'nin'," Aunt Fanny whispered to Aunt Tempe, and Aunt Tempe whispered back, "I reckon he done been in his secut closet an' had a pensacoshul showah befo' he come."

"He sholy been a dwellin' on Mount Sinai. Seem lak he mus a'hyeahed de thundah."

"Heish, honey, he's a thunde'in hisself."

And so like the whisper of waves on a shore, the ripple of comment ran around the meeting house, for there were none present but saw that in some way the spirit had mysteriously descended upon their pastor.

Just as the prayer ended and the congregation had swung into another spiritual hymn, Ike entered with a scared look upon his face and took a seat far back near the door. He glanced sheepishly about the church, and then furtively at Brother Parker. Once he made as if to rise, but thinking better of it, ducked his head and kept his seat.

Now, if one thing more than another was needed to fire the exhorter, it was the voluntary presence of this sinner untouched by the gospel.

The Trousers

His eyes glowed and his old frame quivered with emotion. He would deliver a message that morning that would be pointed straight at the heart of Ike.

To the observer not absorbed by one idea, however, there was something particularly strange in the actions of this last comer. Some things that he did did not seem to argue that he had come to the house of worship seeking a means of grace. After his almost stealthy entrance and his first watchful glances about the room, he had subsided into his seat with an attitude that betokened a despair not wholly spiritual. His eyes followed every motion the preacher made as he rose and looked over the congregation and he grew visibly more uneasy. Once or twice it seemed that the door behind him opened a bit and there is no doubt that several times he turned and looked that way, on one occasion giving his head a quick shake when the door was hastily, but softly closed.

When Parker began his sermon Ike crept guiltily to his feet to slip out, but the old preacher paused with his eyes upon him, saying, "I hope none o' de cong'egation will leave de sanctua'y befo' de sehvice is ended. We is in now, an' gettin' up will distu'b de res.' Hit ain't gwine hu't none of us to gin one day to de Lawd, spechully ef dem what is neah an' deah unto us is layin' erpon de bed of affliction," and the man had sunk back miserably into his seat with the looks of all his fellows fixed on him. From then, he watched the preacher as if fascinated.

Parker was in his glory. He had before him a sinner writhing on the Gospel gridiron and how he did apply the fire.

Ike moved about and squirmed, but the old man held him with his eye while he heaped coals of fire upon the head of the sinner man. He swept the whole congregation with his gaze, but it came back and rested on Ike as he broke into the song,

"Oh, sinnah, you needn't try to run erway,
You sho' to be caught on de jedgment day."

He sung the camp meeting "spiritual" with its powerful personal allusions all through, and then resumed his sermon. "Oh, I tell you de Gospel is a p'inted swo'd to de sinnah. Hit mek him squi'm, hit mek him shivvah and hit mek him shek. He sing loud in de day, but he hide his

" 'I TELL YOU, DE GOSPEL IS A P'INTED SWO'D TO DE
SINNAH' "

face at night. Oh, sinnah, what you gwine to do on de gret day? What do de song say?

'W'en de rocks an' de mountains shell all flee erway,
W'y a you shell have a new hidin' place dat day.'

Oh, sinnah man, is you a huntin' fu' de new hidin' place? Is you a fixin' fu' de time w'en de rocks shell be melted an' de mountains shell run lak rivers?"

Parker had settled well down to his work. As his own people would have expressed it, "He'd done tried de watah an' waded out." They were shouting and crying aloud as he talked. A low minor of moans ran around the room, punctuated by the sharp slapping of hands and stamping of feet. On all sides there were cries of "Truth, truth!" "Amen!" "Amen!" and "Keep in de stream, Pahkah; keep in de stream!"

This encouragement was meat to the pastor's soul and he rose on the wings of his eloquence. The sweat was pouring down his black face. He put his hand back to his pocket to pull out his handkerchief to wipe his face. It came out with a flourish, and with it a pack of cards. They flew into the air, wavered and then fluttered down like a flock of doves. Aces, jacks, queens and tens settled all about the floor grinning wickedly face upward. Parker stopped still in the midst of a sentence and gazed speechless at the guilty things before him. The people gasped. It all flashed over them in a minute. They had heard a story of their pastor's fondness for the devil's picture books in his younger days and now it had come back upon him and he had fallen once more. Here was incontestable proof.

Parker, in a dazed way, put his hand again into his back pocket and brought forth the king of spades. His flock groaned.

"Come down outen dat pulpit," cried one of the bolder ones. "Come down!"

Then Parker found his voice.

"Fo' de lawd, folks," he said, gazing sorrowfully at the king. "Dese ain't my pants ner my cyards." Then his eye fell upon Ike, who was taking advantage of the confusion to make toward the door and he thundered at him. "Come back hyeah, you rapscallion, an' claim yo' dev'ment! Come back hyeah."

Ike came shamefacedly back. He came forward and commenced to pick up the cards while Parker was making his explanations to the relieved flock. The sinner got all of the cards, except one and that one the preacher still held.

"Brothah Pahkah, Brother Pahkah," he whispered, "You's a hol'in' de king." The old man dropped it as if it had burnt him and grabbing it, the scapegrace fled.

Outside the door all things were explained. Several fellows with angry faces were waiting for Ike.

"Couldn't he'p it, boys," he said. "He done begun sehvice w'en I got in. I couldn't stop him, an' den w'en he dropped all the res' he held on to de king."

"Well, all I got to say," said the fiercest of the lot, "don' you nevah put dat deck in yo' pocket no mo' an' len' yo' pants. Come on, de game's been waitin' a houah, put' nigh."

THE LAST FIDDLING OF MOR-
DAUNT'S JIM.

When the Spirit has striven with a man year
after year without success, when he has been con-
victed and then gone back, when he has been con-
verted and then backslidden, it's about time to
say of him that there is the devil's property, with
his deed signed and sealed. All of these things
had happened to Jim. He became serious and
bowed his head in the meeting house, a sure sign
of contrition and religious intention, but the very
next night he had been caught "wingin' " behind
the smoke-house with the rest of the unregenerate. Once he had actually cried out "Amen!"
but it was afterwards found out that one of his
fellows had trodden upon his foot, and that the
"Amen" came in lieu of a less virtuous expletive.

Had it been that Jim's iniquities affected himself only he might have been endured, at least
with greater patience; but this was not so. He
was the prime mover in every bit of deviltry that
set the plantation by the ears, and the most
effectual destroyer of every religious influence
that its master attempted to throw around it.

His one fiddle had caused more backsliding, more flagrant defections from the faith than had any other invention of the devil that the plantation knew.

All of Parker's pleas and sermons had been unavailing—even his supreme exhortation, when he threatened the wicked with eternal fiddling, when their souls should be pining for rest and silence and never find it. Jim was there, but he appeared unmoved. He laughed when Parker broke out, "Fiddle on, you sinnahs, fiddle on! But de time'll come w'en you'll want to hyeah praih, an' you'll hyeah a fiddle; w'en you'll want to sing a hymn, an' you'll hyeah a fiddle; w'en you'll be list'nin' fu' de soun' of de angels' voices erbove de noise of earf, an' you'll hyeah a fiddle. Fiddle on, sinnahs, but w'en you hyeah de soun' of Jerdon a-dashin' on de rocks, w'en you hyeah de watah leapin' an' a-lashin', way up erbove dem all you'll hyeah de devil fiddlin' fu' you an' you'll follah him on an' into dat uttah da'kness whaih dey is wailin' an' gnash-in' o' teef. Fiddle on, sinnah, fiddle on! dance on, sinnah, dance on! laugh on, sinnah, laugh on! but I tell you de time will come w'en dat laughin' will be tu'ned to weepin', an' de soun' of de fiddle shell be as de call of de las' trump in yo' yeahs." And Jim laughed. He went home that night and fiddled until nearly morning.

" 'Pears to me," he said to his wife, "a good fiddle 'ud be a moughty fine t'ing to hyeah ez a body was passin' ovah Jerdon, ez ol' Pahkah calls it."

"Nemmine, Jim," said Mandy, solemn and shocked; "nemmine, you an' yo' dev'ment. Brothah Pahkah right, an' de time gwine come w'en dat fiddle gwine ter be to yo' soul ez a millstone dat been cas' in de middle of de sea, dat'll bring fo'th tares, some fifty an' some a hund'ed fol'. Nemmine, all I got to say to you, you bettah listen to de Wo'd ez it is preached."

"Mandy," said Jim irreverently, "d'you 'membah dat ol' chune, 'Hoe co'n, an' dig pertaters?' Don't it go 'long somep'n' lak dis?"

"Lawsy, yes, honey, dat's hit," and before the poor deluded creature knew what she was doing she was nodding her head in time to the seductive melody, while Jim fiddled and chuckled within himself until the joke was too much for him, and he broke down and ended with a discord which brought Mandy to her sorrowing senses.

Her discretion came to her, though not before

Parker's white inquisitive head had been stuck in at the door.

"Lawd, Sis' Mandy," he cried in dismay, "you ain't collogin' wid de spe'it of de devil, too, is you? Lawd a' mussy, 'pon my soul, an' you one of de faiful of de flock! My soul!"

"I ain't been collogin' wid de devil, Brothah Pahkah," said Mandy contritely, "but dat rapscallion, he fool me an' got my haid to gwine 'fo' I knowed whut I was 'bout."

"Uh, uh, uh," murmured the preacher.

Jim was convulsed. "Hit sho' is a mighty funny 'ligion you preaches, Brothah Pahkah, w'en one fiddle chune kin des' mortally lay out all o' yo' himes."

Parker turned on Jim with the old battle fire in his eyes. "Go on!" he cried. "Go on, but I lay you'll fiddle yo'se'f in hell yit!" And without more ado he stamped away. He was very old, and his temper was shorter than it used to be.

The events of the next week followed each other in quick succession and there are many tales, none fully authenticated, about what really occurred. Some say that, hurt to the quick, Parker tramped around late that night after his visit to Jim's cabin. Others say that he was old and feeble and that his decline was inevitable. Whatever the truth about the cause of it, the old man was taken with a heavy cold which developed into fever. Here, too, chroniclers disagree, for some say that at no time was he out of his head, and that his wild ravings about fiddles and fiddlings were the terrible curses that a righteous man may put, and often does put, on a sinner.

For days the old man's life hung in the balance, and Jim grew contrite under the report of his sufferings and Mandy's accusations. Indeed, he fiddled no more, and the offending "box," as he called it, lay neglected on a shelf.

"Yes, you tryin' to git good now, aftah you mos' nigh killed dat ol' man, havin' him trompin' erroun' in de night aih lookin' aftah yo' dev'-ment." Women are so cruel when they feel themselves in the right.

"He wan't trompin' erroun' aftah me. I ain't nevah sont fu' him," was always Jim's sullen reply.

" 'Tain't no use beatin' erbout de bush; you knows you been causin' dat ol' man a heap er trouble, an' many's de time he mought 'a' been in baid takin' a good res' ef it hadn't been fu' yo' ca'in' on.''

Jim grinned a sickly grin and lapsed into silence. What was the use of arguing with a woman anyway, and how utterly useless it was when the argument happened to be about her preacher! It is really a remarkable thing how, when it comes to woman, the philosophy of man in the highest and lowest grades of life arrives at the same conclusion. So Jim kept his mouth shut for several days until the one on which the news came that Parker had rallied and was ''on the mend;'' then he opened it to guffaw. This brought Mandy down upon him once more.

"I sholy don't know whut to mek o' you, Jim. Instid o' spreadin' dat mouf o' yo'n, you ought to be down on yo' knees a-thankin' de Lawd dat Brothah Pahkah ain't passed ovah an' lef' yo' 'niquities on yo' soul.''

"La, chile, heish up; I's gwine celebrate Brothah Pahkah's 'cov'ry.''

Jim busied himself with dusting and tuning his neglected instrument, and immediately after supper its strains resounded again through the quarters. It rose loud and long, a gladsome sound. What wonder, then, that many of the young people, happy in their old pastor's recovery, should gather before Jim's cabin and foot it gayly there?

But in the midst of the merriment a messenger hastened into the cabin with the intelligence that Brother Parker wanted Jim at his cabin. Something in the messenger's face, or in the tone of his voice, made Jim lay his fiddle aside and hurry to Parker's bedside.

"Howdy, Bud' Jim?" said Parker weakly.

"Howdy, Brothah Pahkah?" said Jim nervously; "how you come on?"

"Well, I's clothed an' in my right min' at las', bless Gawd. Been havin' a little frolic down to yo' cabin to-night?"

Jim twirled his piece of hat tremulously.

"Yes, suh, we was a kin' o' celebratin' yo' gittin' well."

"Dat uz a moughty po' way o' celebratin' fu' me, Jim, but I ain't gwine scol' you now. Dey say dat w'ile I wuz outen my haid I said ha'd tings erbout you an' yo' fiddlin', Jim. An' now dat de Lawd has giv' me my senses back ergin, I want to ax yo' pa'don."

"Brothah Pahkah," Jim interrupted brokenly,

66

"I ain't meant no ha'm to'ds you. Hit des' mus' 'a' been natchul dev'ment in me."

"I ain't a-blamin' you, Jim, I ain't a-blamin' you; I only wanted to baig yo' pa'don fu' whut-evah I said w'en my min' wan't mine."

"You don' need to baig my pa'don."

"Run erlong now, Jim, an' ac' de bes' you kin; so-long."

"So-long, Brothah Pahkah," and the contrite sinner went slowly out and back to the cabin, sorrow, fear, and remorse tugging at his heart.

He went back to his cabin and to bed at once, but he could not sleep for the vague feeling of waiting that held his eyes open and made him start at every sound. An hour passed with him under this nervous tension and then a tap came at the door. He sprang up to open it, and Mandy, as if moved by the same impulse, rose and began to dress hurriedly. Yes, his worst fears were realized. Parker was worse, and they sent for Mandy to nurse him in what they believed to be his last hours.

Jim dressed, too, and for a while stood in the door watching the lights and shadows moving over in the direction of the preacher's cabin. Then an ague seemed to seize him, and with a shiver he came back into the room and closed and bolted the door.

He had sat there, it seemed, a long while, when suddenly out of the stillness of the night a faint sound struck on his ears. It was as if some one far away were fiddling, fiddling a wild, weird tune. Jim sat bolt upright, and the sweat broke out upon his face in great cold drops. He waited. The fiddling came nearer. Jim's lips began moving in silent, but agitated, prayer. Nearer and nearer came the sound, and the face of the scapegrace alone in the cabin turned ashen with fear, then seizing his own fiddle, he smashed it into bits upon the chair, crying the while: "Lawd, Lawd, spaih me, an' I'll nevah fiddle ergin!" He was on his knees now, but the demon of the fiddle came so relentlessly on that he sprang up and hurled himself against the door in a very ecstasy of terror while he babbled prayer on prayer for protection, for just one more trial. Then it seemed that his prayer had been answered. The music began to recede. It grew fainter and fainter and passed on into silence.

Not, however, until the last note had passed away did Jim leave the door and sink helpless on his knees beside the broken fiddle. It seemed ages before he opened the door to Mandy's knock.

"Brothah Pahkah done daid," she said sadly.

"I know it," Jim replied; "I knowed it w'en he died, 'case de devil come fu' me, an' tried to fiddle my soul erway to hell, an' he 'u'd done it, too, ef I hadn't a-wrassled in praih."

"Jim, has you been visited?"

"I has," was the solemn reply, "an' I'll nevah fiddle no mo' ez long ez I live. Daih's de fiddle."

Mandy looked at the broken instrument, and the instinct of thrift drove out her superstition. "Jim," she cried out angrily, "whut you wan' 'o go brek up dat good fiddle fu'? Why'n't you sell it?"

"No, ma'am, no ma'am, I know whut's in dat fiddle. I's been showed, an' I ain't gwine temp' no man wid de devil's inst'ument."

From that moment Jim was a pious man, and at the great funeral which they gave Brother Parker a few days later there was no more serious and devout mourner than he. The whole plantation marveled and the only man who held the key to the situation could not tell the story. He was only a belated serenader who had fiddled to keep up his spirits on a lonely road.

But Parker's work was not without its fruition, for his death accomplished what his life had failed to do, and no more moral story was known or told on the plantation than that of the last fiddling of Mordaunt's Jim.

A SUPPER BY PROXY.

There was an air of suppressed excitement about the whole plantation. The big old house stared gravely out as if it could tell great things if it would, and the cabins in the quarters looked prophetic. The very dogs were on the alert, and there was expectancy even in the eyes of the piccaninnies who rolled in the dust. Something was going to happen. There was no denying that. The wind whispered it to the trees and the trees nodded.

Then there was a clatter of horses' hoofs, the crack of a whip. The bays with the family carriage swept round the drive and halted at the front porch. Julius was on the box, resplendent in his holiday livery. This was the signal for a general awakening. The old house leered an irritating "I told you so." The quarters looked complacent. The dogs ran and barked, the piccaninnies laughed and shouted, the servants gathered on the lawn and, in the midst of it all, the master and mistress came down the steps and got into the carriage. Another crack of the whip, a shout from the servants, more antics

from the piccaninnies, the scurrying of the dogs
—and the vehicle rumbled out of sight behind a
clump of maples. . Immediately the big house resumed its natural appearance and the quarters
settled back into whitewashed respectability.

Mr. and Mrs. Mordaunt were off for a week's
visit. The boys were away at school, and here
was the plantation left in charge of the negroes
themselves, except for the presence of an overseer who did not live on the place. The conditions seemed pregnant of many things, but a
calm fell on the place as if every one had decided to be particularly upon his good behavior.
The piccaninnies were subdued. The butlers in
the big house bowed with wonderful deference to
the maids as they passed them in the halls, and
the maids called the butlers "mister" when they
spoke to them. Only now and again from the
fields could a song be heard. All this was
ominous.

By the time that night came many things were
changed. The hilarity of the little darkies had
grown, and although the house servants still remained gravely quiet, on the return of the field
hands the quarters became frankly joyous. From
one cabin to another could be heard the sound of

"Juba, Juba!" and the loud patting of hands and the shuffling of feet. Now and again some voice could be heard rising above the rest, improvising a verse of the song, as:

"Mas' done gone to Philamundelphy, Juba, Juba.
Lef' us bacon, lef' us co'n braid, Juba, Juba.
Oh, Juba dis an' Juba dat, an' Juba skinned de yaller cat
To mek his wife a Sunday hat, Oh, Juba!"

Not long did the sounds continue to issue from isolated points. The people began drifting together, and when a goodly number had gathered at a large cabin, the inevitable thing happened. Some one brought out a banjo and a dance followed.

Meanwhile, from the vantage ground of the big house, the more favored servants looked disdainfully on, and at the same time consulted together. That they should do something to entertain themselves was only right and proper. No one of ordinary intelligence could think for a moment of letting this opportunity slip without taking advantage of it. But a dance such as the quarters had! Bah! They could never think of it. That rude, informal affair! And these black aristocrats turned up their noses. No, theirs must be a grave and dignified affair, such as their master himself would have given, and they would send out invitations to some on the neighboring plantations.

It was Julius, the coachman, who, after winning around the head butler, Anderson, insisted that they ought to give a grand supper. Julius would have gone on without the butler's consent had it not been that Anderson carried the keys. So the matter was canvassed and settled.

The next business was the invitations, but no one could write. Still, this was a slight matter; for neatly folded envelopes were carried about to the different favored ones, containing—nothing, while at the same time the invitations were proffered by word of mouth.

"Hi, dah!" cried Jim to Julius on the evening that the cards had been distributed; "I ain't seed my imbitation yit."

"You needn't keep yo' eyes bucked looking fu' none, neithah," replied Julius.

"Uh, puttin' on airs, is you?"

"I don't caih to convuss wid you jest now," said Julius pompously.

A Supper by Proxy

Jim guffawed. "Well, of all de sights I evah seed, a dahky coachman offen de box tryin' to look lak he on it! Go 'long, Julius, er you'll sholy kill me, man."

The coachman strode on with angry dignity.

It had been announced that the supper was to be a "ladies' an' gent'men's pahty," and so but few from the quarters were asked. The quarters were naturally angry and a bit envious, for they were but human and not yet intelligent enough to recognize the vast social gulf that yawned between the blacks at the "big house" and the blacks who were quartered in the cabins.

The night of the grand affair arrived, and the Mordaunt mansion was as resplendent as it had ever been for one of the master's festivities. The drawing-rooms were gayly festooned, and the long dining-room was a blaze of light from the wax candles that shone on the glory of the Mordaunt plate. Nothing but the best had satisfied Julius and Anderson. By nine o'clock the outside guests began to arrive. They were the dark aristocrats of the region. It was a well-dressed assembly, too. Plump brown arms lay against the dainty folds of gleaming muslin, and white-stocked, brass-buttoned black counterparts of their masters strode up the walks. There were Dudley Stone's Gideon and Martha, Robert Curtis' Ike with Dely, and there were Quinn, and Doshy, and, over them all, Aunt Tempe to keep them straight. Of these was the company that sat down to Stuart Mordaunt's board.

After some rivalry, Anderson held the head of the table, while Julius was appeased by being placed on the right beside his favorite lady. Aunt Tempe was opposite the host where she could reprove any unseemly levity or tendency to skylarking on the part of the young people. No state dinner ever began with more dignity. The conversation was nothing less than stately, and everybody bowed to everybody else every time they thought about it. This condition of affairs obtained through the soup. Somebody ventured a joke and there was even a light laugh during the fish. By the advent of the entree the tongues of the assembly had loosened up, and their laughter had melted and flowed as freely as Stuart Mordaunt's wine.

"Well, I mus say, Mistah An'erson, dis is sholy a mos' salub'ious occasion."

"Thank you, Mistah Cu'tis, thank you; it ah allus my endeavoh to mek my gues'es feel deyse'ves at home. Let me give you some mo' of dis wine. It's f'om de bes' dat's in my cellah."

"Seems lak I remembah de vintage," said Ike, sipping slowly and with the air of a connoisseur.

"Oh, yes, you drinked some o' dis on de 'casion of my darter's ma'ige to Mas'—to Mistah Daniels."

"I ricollec', yes, I ricollec'."

"Des lis'en at dem dahkies," said the voice of a listening field hand.

Gideon, as was his wont, was saying deeply serious things to Martha, and Quinn whispered something in Doshy's ear that made her giggle hysterically and cry: "Now, Mr. Quinn, ain't you scan'lous? You des seem lak you possessed dis evenin'."

In due time, however, the ladies withdrew, and the gentlemen were left over their cigars and cognac. It was then that one of the boys detailed to wait on the table came in and announced to the host that a tramp was without begging for something to eat. At the same instant the straggler's face appeared at the door, a poor, unkempt-looking white fellow with a very dirty face. Anderson cast a look over his shoulder at him and commanded pompously:

"Tek him to de kitchen an' give him all he wants."

The fellow went away very humbly.

In a few minutes Aunt Tempe opened the dining-room door and came in.

"An'erson," she cried in a whisper.

"Madam," said the butler rising in dignity, "excuse me—but——"

"Hyeah, don't you come no foo'ishness wid me; I ain't no madam. I's tiahed playing fine lady. I done been out to de kitchen, an' I don' lak dat tramp's face an' fo'm."

"Well, madam," said Anderson urbanely, "we haven't asked you to ma'y him."

At this there was a burst of laughter from the table.

"Nemmine, nemmine, I tell you, I don' lak dat tramp's face an' fo'm, an' you'd bettah keep yo' eye skinned, er you'll be laughin' on de othah side o' yo' mouf."

The butler gently pushed the old lady out, but as the door closed behind her she was still saying, "I don' lak dat tramp's face an' fo'm."

Unused to playing fine lady so long, Aunt Tempe deserted her charges and went back to the kitchen, but the "straggler man" had gone.

A Supper by Proxy

It is a good thing she did not go around the veranda, where the windows of the dining-room opened, or she would have been considerably disturbed to see the tramp peeping through the blinds—evidently at the Mordaunt plate that sparkled conspicuously on the table.

Anderson with his hand in his coat, quite after the manner of Stuart Mordaunt, made a brief speech in which he thanked his guests for the honor they had done him in coming to his humble home. "I know," he said, "I have done my po' bes'; but at some latah day I hopes to entertain you in a mannah dat de position an' character of de gent'men hyeah assembled desuves. Let us now jine de ladies."

His hand was on the door and all the gentlemen were on their feet when suddenly the window was thrown up and in stepped the straggler.

"W'y, w'y, how daih you, suh, invade my p'emises?" asked Anderson, casting a withering glance at the intruder, who stood gazing around him.

"Leave de room dis minute!" cried Julius, anxious to be in the fray. But the tramp's eyes were fastened on Anderson. Finally he raised one finger and pointed at him.

"You old scoundrel," he said in a well-known voice, as he snatched off his beard and wig and threw aside his disguising duster and stood before them.

"Mas' Stu'at!"

"You old scoundrel, you! I've caught you, have I?"

Anderson was speechless and transfixed, but the others were not, and they had cleared that room before the master's linen duster was well off. In a moment the shuffling of feet ceased and the lights went out in the parlor. The two stood there alone, facing each other.

"Mas' Stu'at."

"Silence," said Mordaunt, raising his hand, and taking a step toward the trembling culprit.

"Don' hit me now, Mas' Stu'at, don' hit me ontwell I's kin' o' shuk off yo' pussonality. Ef you do, it'll be des' de same ez thumpin yo'se'f."

Mordaunt turned quickly and stood for a moment looking through the window, but his shoulders shook.

"Well," he said, turning; "do you think you've at last relieved yourself of my personality?"

"I don't know, I don't know. De gyahment sho' do fit monst'ous tight."

" ' YOU OLD SCOUNDREL,' SAID A WELL KNOWN VOICE "

"Humph. You take my food, you take my wine, you take my cigars, and now even my personality isn't safe.

"Look here, what on earth do you mean by entertaining half the darkies in the county in my dining-room?"

Anderson scratched his head and thought. Then he said: "Well, look hyeah, Mas' Stu'at, dis hyeah wasn't rightly my suppah noways."

"Not your supper! Whose was it!"

"Yo'n."

"Mine?"

"Yes, suh."

"Why, what's the matter with you, Anderson? Next thing you'll be telling me that I planned it all, and invited all those servants."

"Lemme 'splain it, Mas', lemme 'splain it. Now I didn't give dat suppah as An'erson. I give it ez Mas' Stu'at Mordaunt; an' Quinn an' Ike an' Gidjon, dey didn't come fu' deyse'ves, dey come fu' Mas' Cu'tis, an' Mas' Dudley Stone. Don' you un'erstan', Mas' Stu'at? We wasn' we-all, we was you-all."

"That's very plain; and in other words, I gave a supper by proxy, and all my friends responded in the same manner?"

"Well, ef dat means what I said, dat's it."

"Your reasoning is extremely profound, Anderson. It does you great credit, but if I followed your plan I should give you the thrashing you deserve by proxy. That would just suit you. So instead of that I am going to feed you, for the next day or so, by that ingenious method. You go down and tell Jim that I want him up here early to-morrow morning to eat your breakfast."

"Oh, Mas' Stu'at! Whup me, whup me, but don't tell dose dahkies in de quahtahs, an' don't sta've me!" For Anderson loved the good things of life.

"Go."

Anderson went, and Mordaunt gave himself up to mirth.

The quarters got their laugh out of Anderson's discomfiture. Jim lived high for a day, but rumors from the kitchen say that the butler did not really suffer on account of his supper by proxy.

THE TROUBLE ABOUT SOPHINY.

Always on the plantation there had been rivalry between Julius, the coachman, and Anderson, the butler, for social leadership. Mostly it had been good-natured, with now and then a somewhat sharper contest when occasion demanded it. Mostly, too, Anderson had come off victorious on account of certain emoluments, honestly or dishonestly come by, that followed his position. Now, however, they were at loggerheads and there seemed no possible way to settle the matter in the usual amicable manner. Anderson swore dire things against Julius, and the latter would be satisfied with nothing less than his enemy's destruction. There was no use in the peacemakers on the plantation trying to bring them together. They were sworn enemies and would have none of it. In fact, there was no way to adjudicate the affair, for it concerned no less a matter than who should have the right to take Miss Sophiny to the great ball that was to be given in her honor.

Perhaps you do not know that Miss Sophiny was maid to Mistress Fairfax, who was now on a visit to the Mordaunt plantation, and in the whole State the prettiest girl, black, brown, or yellow that had ever tossed her head, imitated her mistress and set her admirers wild. She was that entrancing color between brown and yellow which is light brown if you are pleasant and gingerbread if you want to hurt a body's feelings. Also, Sophiny had lustrous, big black eyes that had learned from her mistress the trick of being tender or languishing at their owner's will.

Mistress Fairfax and her maid had not been on the grounds a day before they had disrupted the whole plantation.

From the very first, Julius had paid the brown damsel devoted court. In fact, as the coachman, he had driven up from the station with her mistress and had the first chance to show her his gallantry. It is true that Anderson came into the lists immediately after, and found a dainty for her even before he had served her mistress, but it could not be denied that he was after Julius, and it was upon his priority of attention that the coachman based his claim to present precedence.

For days the contest between the two men was pretty balanced. Julius walked down the quarters' road with her, but Anderson stood talking with her on the back veranda for nearly an hour. She went to the stables with the coachman to look over the horses, in which he took a special pride; but she dropped into the butler's pantry to try his latest confection. She laughed at a joke by Julius, but said "You're right" to a wise remark that Anderson made. Altogether, their honors seemed dangerously even.

Then the big house gave the grand ball for Mistress Fairfax, and the servants' quarters could hardly wait to follow their example in giving something for the maid. It was here that the trouble arose. Their ball was to be a great affair. It was to be given in the largest of the cabins, and field and house were to unite to do honor to the fair one. But the question was: Who was to have the honor of escorting her to the ball?

Now it might be supposed that under ordinary circumstances such a matter would be left to the personal preference of the lady most concerned; but that is just where the observer makes his first mistake. His premise is wrong. This was no ordinary matter. Had the lady shown any decided preference for either one or the other of

her suitors; had either even the shade of a hair
an advantage over the other, it would all have
been different. It would have resolved itself
merely into a trial of personal influence and the
vanquished would have laughed with his victor.
But it was not so. Miss Sophiny had treated
them both painfully alike. The one who took
the lady would gain a distinct advantage over
his fellow, and this must not be left to chance.
They must settle outside their charmer's knowledge once and for all as to which should ask and,
as a consequence, be her escort.

Now it was at this time that the mirth-loving
master, Stuart Mordaunt, took note of the affair.
He saw that there was bad feeling between his
butler and his coachman, and he was not long in
finding out the cause thereof. There were many
with the story waiting on their lips and anxious
to tell him. The little tale filled Mordaunt with
mischievous joy. He hurried to the house with
the news that there was trouble on the plantation.

"Look a-here, Miss Caroline," he said to his
visitor, "I had no idea your coming was going
to cause such a commotion on my place. Why, I
really believe that I'm threatened with an upris-

ing, and all about that maid of yours. It's really doubtful whether we shall be able to drive any-where, and I am beginning to tremble for the serving of my meals, for all the trouble seems to center in my coachman and my butler."

"Now, tell me, Mr. Stuart, what has that girl been doing now? Honestly, she's the plague of my life."

"Oh, no more than her mistress did last winter down at the capitol. It's really remarkable what a lot of human nature horses and niggers have."

"Aren't you ashamed of yourself, Mr. Mordaunt? Pray, what did I do last winter at the capitol?"

"The whole case is as bad as it was between Captain Carter and Willis Breckinridge, and I'm expecting the affair of honor between Julius and Anderson at any time. If you hear the sudden report of pistols you may all just know what it is and thank your maid Sophiny for bringing it about."

Miss Caroline laughed heartily at her host's bantering, but he went on in a tone of mock seriousness, "You may laugh, now, my lady, but I'll warrant you'll sing another tune if you have to go walking about this place or perchance have to set to work some of you and get your own dinners; and that's what it will come to if this matter goes on much longer."

The rivalry between the two servants had now run its course for some time, and as neither man seemed disposed to yield, it threatened to ruin the whole entertainment, which had been postponed from time to time to allow of an adjustment of the matter. Finally, when that night of pleasure was too visibly menaced, Jim, the unregenerate, came forward with a solution of the problem. "Why," he argued, "should Julius and Anderson be allowed to spoil the good time of the whole plantation by their personal disagreements and bickerings? What was it to the rest of them, who took Miss Sophiny, so she came and they had their dance? If the two must differ, why not differ like men and fight it out? Then, the one that whipped had the right to take the young lady." Jim was primitive. He was very close to nature. He did not argue it out in just these words, but his fellows took his meaning, and they said, "That's so."

Now, neither Julius nor Anderson much favored the idea of fighting. Each wanted to save himself and look his best on the momentous night. But the fact that unless the matter were soon settled there would be no such night, and because the force of opinion all around pressed them, they accepted Jim's solution of the problem and decided to fight out their differences.

Meanwhile there was an unholy twinkle in the eye of Miss Sophiny. She was not unmindful of all that was going on, but she kept her counsel.

Neither Julius nor his fellow servant was in particularly good fighting trim. One had been stiffened by long hours, both in winter and summer upon the carriage. The other had been softened by being much in the house and by over feeding. But as their disadvantages were equal these could not justly be taken into account and so are passed over.

As the plantation was manifesting a growing impatience for its festivities and the visitor's stay was drawing to a close, they set the time for the encounter on the night after the matter was proposed. It was soon, but not too soon for some solicitous one to inform the master of what was going on.

The place chosen was one remote from the big house and behind an old dismantled smoke-house in which the card games were usually played of a Sunday. At the appointed time, the few who were in the secret gathered and formed a ring about the rivals, who faced each other stripped to the waist. There was not a great show of confidence or eagerness in their bearing, and there would have been less could they have known that their master with Miss Caroline and several members of the family were hiding just around the corner of the smoke-house, convulsed with laughter.

The two men were a funny sight as they stood there in the ring fearfully facing each other. Julius was tall and raw-boned, while Anderson was short and fat from much feeding. When the preliminaries were all arranged the fight began without further ceremony. Julius led with a heavy awkward blow that caught his opponent just above where the belt should have been, and Anderson grunted with a sound like a half-filled barrel. This was enough. The blow was immediately returned by the butler's bending his head and butting his rival quickly and resoundingly. Before he could recover his upright position, however, the tall coachman had caught him under his arm and was trying to work havoc on his woolly pate. For a few minutes they danced around in this position, for all the world like two roosters when one shields his head under the other's wing.

"Brek aloose," cried Jim, excitedly, "brek aloose, dat ain't no fist fightin'."

The men separated and began to pummel each other at a distance and in good earnest. Anderson's nose was bleeding, and Julius' eye was closed to earthly scenes. They were both panting like engines.

At this juncture, thinking it had gone far enough, Mordaunt, with much ado to keep his face straight, emerged from behind the smokehouse. At first the combatants did not see him, so busily were they engaged, but the sound of scurrying feet as their spectators fled the scene, called them to themselves and they turned to meet the eyes of their master fixed upon them with a sternness that it was all he could do to maintain.

"Well, you are a pretty pair. Here, what is the meaning of this?"

The two men hung their heads. A giggle, pretty well-defined, came from behind the smoke-house, and they became aware that their master was not alone. They were covered with confusion.

"Get into your coats." They hustled into their garments. "Now tell me what is the meaning of this?"

"We was des' a fightin' a little," said Julius, sheepishly.

"Just for fun, I suppose?"

No answer.

"I say, just for fun?"

"Well, I seen huh fust," Julius broke out like a big boy.

"Don' keer ef yo' did, I did mo' talkin' to huh, an' I got de right to tek huh to th' pa'ty, dat's what I have."

"Well, you're a pretty pair," repeated the master. "Has it ever occurred to you that Sophiny herself might have something to say as to who went with her?"

"Well, dat's des' what I say, but Julius he want to ax huh fus' an' so does I."

"Anderson, I'm ashamed of you. Why ain't you got sense enough to go together and ask her, and so settle the matter peacefully? If it wasn't for the rest of the hands you should not have any dance at all. Now take yourselves to the house and don't let me hear any more of this business."

Mordaunt turned quickly on his heel as the combatants slipped away. His gravity had stood all that it could. As soon as he had joined the others he broke into a peal of laughter in which Miss Caroline and the rest joined him.

"Oh, you women," he exclaimed, "didn't I warn you that we should have an affair of honor on our hands? It's worse, positively worse than Carter and Breckinridge."

"Yes, it is worse," assented Miss Caroline, mischievously, "for in this encounter some blood was drawn," and they took their way merrily to the house.

Julius and Anderson were both glad of the relief that their master had brought to them and of the expedient he had urged for getting around their difficulty. They talked amicably of the plan as they pursued their way.

"I'll go fix my eye an' yo' ten' to yo' nose, an' den we'll go an' see Miss Sophiny togethah des' lak Mas' says."

"All right, I'll be ready in a minute."

When they had somewhat repaired the damage to their countenances the coachman and the butler together set out to find the object of their hearts' desire. Together, each one fearing to let the other talk too much, they laid their case before her.

Sophiny sat on the step of the back porch and swung one slender foot temptingly down and outward. She listened to them with a smile on her face. When they were through she laughed lightly and said, "Why, la, gentlemen, I done p'omised Mistah Sam long 'go. He axed me soon's he hyeahed 'bout it!" Then she laughed again.

Sam was a big field hand and not at all in the coachman's and the butler's social set. They turned away from the siren in silence and when they were some distance off they solemnly shook hands.

MR. GROBY'S SLIPPERY GIFT.

Two men could hardly have been more unlike than Jim and Joe Mordaunt, and when it is considered that they were brothers brought up under the same conditions and trained by the same hand, this dissimilarity seems nothing less than remarkable. Jim was the older, and a better, steadier-going hand Stuart Mordaunt did not own upon the place, while a lazier, more unreliable scamp than Joe could not have been found within a radius of fifty miles.

The former was the leader in all good works, while the latter was at the head of every bit of deviltry that harassed the plantation. Every one recognized the difference between these two, and they themselves did not ignore it.

"Jim, he's de 'ligious pa't o' de fambly," Joe used to say, "an' I's most o' de res' o' it." He looked upon his brother with a sort of patronizing condescension, as if his own wickedness in some manner dignified him; but nevertheless, the two were bound together by a rough but strong affection. The wicked one had once almost whipped a fellow-servant to death for saying

95

that his brother couldn't out-pray the preacher.
They were both field hands, and while Jim went
his way and did his work rejoicing, Joe was the
bane of the overseer's life. He would seize every
possible chance of shirking, and it was his standing boast that he worked less and ate more than
any other man on the place.

It was especially irritating to his master, because he was a fine-appearing fellow, with arms
like steel bars, and the strength of a giant. It
was this strength and a certain reckless spirit
about him that kept the overseer from laying
the lash to his back. It was better to let Joe
shirk than to make him desperate, thought Mr.
Groby. In his employer's dilemma, however, he
suggested starvation as a very salutary measure,
but was met with such an angry response that he
immediately apologized. Stuart Mordaunt,
while rejecting his employee's methods, yet
looked to him to work an amendment in Joe's
career. "For," said he, "that rascal will corrupt
the whole plantation. Joe literally carries out
the idea that he doesn't have to work, and is
there a servant on the place who will work if he
thinks he doesn't have to?"

"Yes, one—Joe's brother Jim," said the over-

seer, grinning. "He's what a nigger ought to be
—as steady and as tireless as an ox."

"It's a wonder that brother of his hasn't corrupted him."

"Jim ain't got sense enough to be corrupted
as long as he gets his feed."

"Maybe he's got too much sense," returned
the master coldly. "But do you think that Joe
really has notions?"

"Notions of freedom? No. He's like a balky
horse. He'll stand in his tracks until you beat
the life out of him, but he isn't the kind to run
away. It would take too much exertion."

"I wish to Heaven he would run off!" said
Mordaunt impatiently. "It would save me a
deal of trouble. I don't want to deal harshly
with him, but neither do I want the whole plantation stirred up."

"Why don't you sell him?"

Stuart Mordaunt's eyes flashed up at the overseer as he replied: "I haven't got down to selling my niggers down the river yet."

"Needn't sell him down the river. Sell him
——"

"I'm no nigger-trader," the gentleman broke
in.

"Listen to me," said Mr. Groby, insinuatingly. "My wife wants a good servant up at our house, and I'd be willing to take Joe off your hands. I think I could manage him." He looked for the moment as if he might manage the slave to the poor fellow's sorrow.

"But would you keep him right about here so that I could look after him if he got into trouble?"

"Certainly," said Mr. Groby, jingling the coins in his pocket.

"Then I'll give him to you," said Mordaunt coldly.

"I don't ask that; I——"

"I do not sell, I believe I told you. I'll give him to you."

The overseer laughed quietly when his employer was gone. "Oh, yes," he said to himself, "I think I can manage Joe when he's mine."

"I don't believe I ought to have done that," mused the master as he went his way.

Joe did not know what had happened until the papers transferring him were made out and Groby came and read them to him.

"You see, Joe," he said, "you're mine. I've wanted you for a long time. I've always thought that if you belonged to me I could make a good hand out of you. You see, Joe, I've got no sentiments. Of course you don't know what sentiments are, but you'll understand later. I feel as if I can increase your worth to the world," and Mr. Groby rubbed his hands and smiled.

The black man said nothing, but at night, humble and pleading, he went to see his old master. When Stuart Mordaunt saw him coming he did not feel altogether easy in his mind, but he tried to comfort himself by affecting to believe that Joe would be pleased.

"Well, Joe," he said, "I suppose you'll be glad to get away from the field?"

"Glad to git erway—oh, mastah!" He suddenly knelt and threw his arms about his master's knees. "Oh, Mas' Stua't," he cried, "don' gi' me to dat Mistah Groby; don' do it! I want to wo'k fu' you all de days o' my life. Don' gi' me to dat man!"

"Why, Joe, you never have been anxious before to work for me."

"Mas' Stua't, I knows I ain' been doin' right. I ain' been wo'kin', but I will wo'k. I'll dig my fingahs to de bone; but don' gi' me to dat man."

99

'But, Joe, you don't understand. You'll have a good home, easier work, and more time to yourself—almost the same as if you were up to the big house."

This was every field-hand's ambition, and Stuart Mordaunt thought that his argument would silence the refractory servant, but Joe was not to be silenced so. He raised his head and his black face was twitching with emotion. "I'd ravver be yo' fiel'-han' dan dat man Groby's mastah."

Mordaunt was touched, but his determination was not altered. "But he'll be good to you, don't you know that?"

"Good to me, good to me! Mas' Stua't, you don' know dat man!"

The master turned away. He had a certain discipline to keep on his place, and he knew it. "Perhaps I don't know him," he said, "but what I don't see with my own eyes I can't spy out with the eyes of my servants. Joe, you may go. I have given my word, and I could not go back even if I would. Be a good boy and you'll get along all right. Come to see me often."

The black man seized his master's hand and pressed it. Great fellow as he was, when he left he was sobbing like a child. He was to stay in the quarters that night and the next morning leave the fields and enter the service of Mrs. Groby.

It was a sad time for him. As he sat by the hearth, his face bowed in his hands, Jim reached over and slapped him on the head. It was as near to an expression of affection and sympathy as he could come. But his brother looked up with the tears shining in his eyes, and Jim, taking his pipe from his mouth, passed it over in silence, and they sat brooding until Mely took a piece of "middlin' " off the coals for brother Joe.

When she had gone to bed the two men talked long, but it was not until she was snoring contentedly and the dogs were howling in the yard and the moon had gone down behind the trees that Mr. Groby's acquisition slipped out of the cabin and away to the woods, bearing with him his brother's blessing and breakfast.

It was near eleven o'clock the next morning when the overseer came to the big house, fuming and waving his papers in his hands. He was looking for his slave. But the big house did not know where he was any more than did the quarters, and he went away disappointed and furious.

Joe had rebelled. He had called the dark night to his aid and it had swallowed him up.

Against Mordaunt's remonstrances, the new-made master insisted upon putting the hounds on the negro's track; but they came back baffled. Joe knew Mr. Groby's methods and had prepared for them.

"It was a slippery gift you gave me, Mr. Mordaunt," said the overseer on the third day after Joe's escape.

"Even a slippery gift shouldn't get out of rough hands, Groby," answered Mordaunt, "and from what I hear your hands are rough enough."

"And they'd be rougher now if I had that black whelp here."

"I'm glad Joe's gone," mused Stuart Mordaunt as he looked at the overseer's retreating figure. "He was lazy and devilish, but Groby ——"

It was just after that that Parker, the plantation exhorter, reported the backsliding of Jim. His first fall from grace consisted in his going to a dance. This was bad enough, but what was worse, although the festivities closed at midnight, Jim—and his wife Mely told it, too—did not reach his cabin until nearly daylight. Of course she was uneasy about it. That was quite natural. There were so many dashing girls on the plantations, within a radius of ten or twelve miles, that no woman's husband was safe. So she went to the minister about it, as women will about their troubles, and the minister went to his master.

"Let him alone," said Stuart Mordaunt. "His brother's absence has upset him, but Jim'll come round all right."

"But, mastah," said old Parker, pushing back his bone-bowed spectacles, "dat uz mighty late fu' Jim to be gittin' in—nigh daylight—ez stiddy a man ez he is. Don't you reckon dey's a 'ooman in it?"

"Look here, Parker," said his master; "aren't you ashamed of yourself? Have you ever known Jim to go with any other woman than Mely? If you preachers weren't such rascals yourselves and married less frequently you wouldn't be so ready to suspect other men."

"Ahem!" coughed Parker. "Well, Mas' Stua't, ef you gwineter question inter de p'ogatives o' de ministry, I'd bettah be gwine, case you on dang'ous groun'," and he went his way.

But even an indulgent master's patience must wear out when a usually good servant lapses into unusually bad habits. Jim was often absent from the plantation now, and things began to disappear: chickens, ducks, geese, and even Jim's own family bacon, and now and then a shoat of the master's found its way off the place.

The thefts could be traced to but one source. Mely didn't mind the shoats, nor the ducks, nor the geese, nor the chickens—they were her master's, and he could afford to lose them—but that her husband should steal hers and the children's food—it was unspeakable. She caught him red-handed once, stealing away with a side of bacon, and she upbraided him loud and long.

"Oh, you low-down scoun'el," she screamed, "stealin' de braid outen yo' chillun's moufs fu' some othah 'ooman!"

Jim, a man of few words, stood silent and abashed, and his very silence drove her to desperation. She went to her master, and the next day the culprit was called up.

"Jim," said Mordaunt, "I want to be as easy with you as I can. You've always been a good servant, and I believe that it's your brother's doings that have got you off the handle. But

Mr. Groby's Slippery Gift

I've borne with you week after week, and I can't stand it any longer. So mark my words: if I hear another complaint I'll have you skinned; do you hear me?"

"Yes, suh."

That night Jim stole a ham from the kitchen before Aunt Doshy's very eyes. When they told the master in the morning he was furious. He ordered that the thief be brought before him, and two whippers with stout corded lashes in their hands stood over the black man's back.

"What's the matter with you, anyhow?" roared Mordaunt. "Are you bound to defy me?"

Jim did not answer.

"Will you answer me?" cried the master.

Still Jim was silent.

"Who is this woman you're stealing for?"

"Ain't stealin' fu' no ooman."

"Don't lie to me. Will you tell?"

Silence.

"Do you hear me? Lay it on him! I'll see whether he'll talk!"

The lashes rose in the air and whizzed down. They rose again, but stopped poised as a gaunt figure coming from nowhere, it seemed, stalked up and pushed the whippers aside.

"Give it to me," said Joe, taking off his coat. "I told him jes' how it would be, an' I was comin' in to gi' myse'f up anyhow. He done it all to keep me f'om sta'vin'; but I's done hidin' now. I'll be dat Groby's slave ravver dan let him tek my blows." He ceased speaking and slipped out of his ragged shirt. " 'Tain't no use, Jim," he added, "you's done all you could."

"Dah, now, Joe," said his brother in disgust, "you's done come hyeah an' sp'iled evaht'ing; you nevah did know yo' place."

"Whup away," said Joe.

But the master's hand went up.

"Joe!" he cried. "Jim, you—you've been taking that food to him! Why didn't you tell me?" He kicked each one of the whippers solemnly, then he kicked Joe. "Get out of this," he said. "You'll be nobody's but mine. I'll buy you from Groby, you low-down, no-account scoundrel." Then he turned and looked down on Jim. "Oh, you fool nigger—God bless you."

When Mr. Groby heard of Joe's return he hastened up to the big house. He was elated.

"Ha," he said, "my man has returned."

Stuart Mordaunt looked unpleasant, then he said: "Your man, Mr. Groby, your man, as you call him, has returned. He is here. But, sir, your man has been redeemed by his brother's vicarious suffering, and I intend—I intend to buy Joe back. Please name your price."

And Mr. Groby saw the look in the gentleman's eye and made his price low.

ASH-CAKE HANNAH AND HER BEN.

Christmas Eve had come, and the cold, keen air with just a hint of dampness in it gave promise of the blessing of a white Christmas. A few flakes began sifting slowly down, and at sight of them a dozen pairs of white eyes flashed, and a dozen negro hearts beat more quickly. It was not long before the sound of grinding axes was heard and the dogs barked a chorus to the grindstones' song, for they, wise fellows that they were, knew what the bright glint of the steel meant. They knew, too, why Jake and Ike and Joe whistled so merrily, and looked over at the distant woods with half-shut eyes and smiled.

Already the overseers were relaxing their vigilance, the quarters were falling into indolence, and the master was guarding the key of a well-filled closet.

Negro Tom was tuning up his fiddle in the barn, and Blophus, with his banjo, was getting the chords from him, while Alec was away out in the woods with his face turned up to the gray sky, letting the kinks out of his tenor voice. All this because the night was coming on. Christmas

Ash-Cake Hannah and Her Ben

Eve night was the beginning of a week of joy.
The wind freshened and the snow fell faster.
The walks were covered. Old gnarled logs that
had lain about, black and forbidding, became
things of beauty. The world was a white glory.
Slowly, so slowly for a winter's night, the lights
faded out and the lamps and candles and torches
like lowly stars laughed from the windows of
big house and cabin. In fireplaces great and
small the hickory crackled, and the savory smell
of cooking arose, tempting, persistent. The
lights at the big house winked at the cabin, and
the cabin windows winked back again. Laughter trickled down the night and good cheer was
everywhere. Everywhere, save in one room,
where Hannah—Ash-Cake Hannah, they called
her—sat alone by her smouldering hearth, brushing the cinders from her fresh-baked cake, mumbling to herself.

For her there was no Christmas cheer. There
were only her dim, lonely cabin and the ash-cov-
ered hearth. While the others rejoiced she
moaned, for she had taken as a husband a slave
on a distant plantation, whose master was a hard
man, and on many a Christmas he had refused
permission to Ben to go and see his wife. So

each year, as soon as Christmas Eve came, Hannah began to mope and fast, eating nothing but ash-cake until she knew whether or not Ben was coming. If he came, she turned to and laughed and made merry with the rest. If he did not, her sorrow and meagre fare lasted the week out, and she went back to her work with a heavy heart and no store of brightness for the coming year. To-day she sat, as usual, mumbling and moaning, for the night was drawing down, and no sign of Ben.

Outside the negroes from the quarters, dressed in their best, were gathering into line, two by two, to march to the big house, where every Christmas they received their presents. There was much pushing and giggling, with ever and anon an admonitory word from one of the older heads, as they caught some fellow's arm making free with a girl's waist. Finally, when darkness had completely come, they started briskly away to the tune of a marching song. As they neared and passed Hannah's cabin they lowered their voices out of respect to the sorrow they knew she was undergoing. But once beyond it they broke out with fresh gusto, stamping or tripping along through the damp snow like so many happy children. Then, as they neared the steps of the great house, the doors were thrown wide and a flood of yellow light flowed out upon the throng of eager faces. With their halting the marching song was stopped, and instantly a mellow voice swung into a Christmas hymn, one of their own rude spirituals:

Oh, moughty day at Bethlehem,
Who dat layin' in de manger?
De town, hit full, dey ain't no room;
Who dat layin' in de manger?

The old master had come forward to the front of the piazza and around him clustered his family and guests, listening with admiration to the full, rich chorus. When it was done the negroes filed through the hall, one by one, each with a "Me'y Chris'mus" and each receiving some token from the master and mistress. Laughing, joking, bantering, they went out to their holidays, some to their cabins to dance or eat, others to the woods with the dogs and the newly sharpened axes to look for game. One of the women stopped at Hannah's cabin with the gift for which she so seldom came. At her knock the lone watcher sprang up and flung the door wide, but sank down again with a groan at sight of the visitor. She did not even open the things which the messenger laid upon the bed, but bent again over her cheerless hearth.

The sound of merriment and song were dying away within the neighboring huts when her door was thrown suddenly open again and a huge negro stood before Ash-Cake Hannah. The slightly nibbled cake was hurled into a dark corner, and the woman sprang up with a heart-cry: "Ben!" She threw her arms about his neck and burst into happy tears, while Ben held her, grinned sheepishly, and kept glancing furtively toward the door.

" 'Sh, 'sh," he said.

"What I want o' 'sh fu', w'en you's hyeah, Ben? I got a min' to hollah," she answered, laughing and crying.

" 'Sh, 'sh," he repeated; "I's run off."

She stopped, and stood staring at him with wide, scared eyes.

"You's run off?" she echoed.

"Yes, Mas' Mason wouldn't let me come, so I tuk my chanst an' come anyhow."

"Oh, Ben, he'll mos' nigh kill you."

"I knows it, but I don' keer. It 'uz Chris'mus an' I was boun' to see you."

"'—AND THE WOMAN SPRANG UP WITH A
HEART-CRY : 'BEN!'"

The woman fell to crying again, but he patted her shoulder, saying: " 'Tain't no use to cry, Hannah. Hit's des' wastin' time. I got to pay fu' dis runnin' off anyhow, so I'd des' ez well have ez good a time ez I kin while hit las'. Fix me some suppah, an' den we'll go roun' a little an' see de folks."

As they went out the deadened sound of merriment came to them from the cabins.

"I don' know ez I ought to show myse'f des' now," said Ben stealthily, as they neared one of the places where the fun was at its height. "Ef I should tek a notion to go back, I mought git in widout Mas' Mason knowin' I been gone, 'dough he moughty sha'p-eyed."

"Le's des stan' outside hyeah, den, an, hol' han's an' listen; dat'll be enough fu' me, seein' you's hyeah."

They stationed themselves outside a cabin window whose shutter was thrown wide open to admit the air. Here they could see and listen to all that went on within. To them it was like starving within sight of food. Their hearts yearned to be enjoying themselves with their kind. But they only clutched each other's hands the tighter, and stood there in the square of yellow light thrown out by the candles and fat pine torches, drinking in all they could of the forbidden pleasures.

Now they were dancing to the tum-tum of a banjo and the scraping of a fiddle, and Ben's toes tingled to be shuffling. After the dance there would be a supper. Already a well-defined odor was arising from a sort of rude lean-to behind the cabin. The smell was rich and warm and sweet.

"What is dat, Hannah?" asked Ben. "Hit smell monst'ous familiah."

"Hit's sweet 'taters, dat's what it is."

Ben turned on her an agonized look. "Hit's sweet 'taters, an' p——" His lips were pouted to say the word, but it was too much for him. He interrupted himself in an attempt to pronounce that juicy, seductive, unctuous word, "possum," and started for the door, exclaiming: "Come on, Hannah; I'd des' ez well die fu' an ol' sheep ez fu' a lamb;" and in a moment he was being welcomed by the surprised dancers.

Ben and Hannah were soon in the very midst of the gayety.

"No ash-cake fu' Hannah dis Chris'mus!" shouted some one as he passed the happy woman in the dance.

Hannah's voice rang loud and clear through the room as she courtesied to her husband and answered: "No, indeed, honey; Hannah gwine live off'en de fat o' de lan' dis hyeah Chris'mus."

In a little while Fullerton, the master, came to the cabin with some of his friends who wanted to enjoy looking on at the negroes' pleasure. This was the signal for the wildest pranks, the most fantastic dancing and a general period of showing off. The happy-go-lucky people were like so many children released from their tasks. The more loudly their visitors applauded the gayer they became. They clapped their hands, they slapped their knees. They leaped and capered. And among them, no one was lighter-hearted than Ben. He had forgotten what lay in store for him, and his antics kept the room in a roar.

Fullerton had seen him and had expressed the belief that Ben had run away, for Mason Tyler would hardly have let him come without sending with him a pass; but he took it easily, glad to see

Hannah enjoying herself, and no longer forced to moan and fast.

For a brief space the dancers had rested. Then the music struck up again. They had made their "'bejunce" and were swinging corners, when suddenly the clatter of horses' hoofs broke in on the rhythm of the music, which stopped with a discord. The people stood startled and expectant, each in the attitude in which he had stopped. Ben was grinning sheepishly and scraping his foot on the floor. All at once he remembered.

With a cry, Hannah ran across the room and threw herself at her master's feet. "Oh, Mas' Jack," she begged, "don' let Mas' Mason Tyler whup Ben! He runned off to be wid me."

"'Sh," said Fullerton quickly; "I'll do what I can."

In another moment the door was flung open and Mason Tyler, a big, gruff-looking fellow with a face red with anger, stood in the doorway. Over his shoulder peeped two negroes. He had a stout whip in his hand.

"Is my—oh, there you are, you black hound. Come here; I'm going to larrup you within an inch of your life."

"Good evening, Mr. Tyler," broke in Fullerton's smooth voice.

"Oh, good-evening, Mr. Fullerton. You must excuse me; I was so taken up with that black hound that I forgot my manners."

Fullerton proceeded to introduce his friends. Tyler met them gruffly.

"Ben, here," he proceeded, "has taken it into his head that he is his own master."

"Oh, well, these things will happen about Christmas time, and you must overlook them."

"Nobody need tell me how to run my place."

"Certainly not, but I've a sort of interest in Ben on Hannah's account. However, we won't talk of it. Come to the house, and let me offer you some refreshment."

"I haven't time."

"My friends will think very badly of you if you don't join us in one holiday glass at least."

Tyler's eyes glistened. He loved his glass. He turned irresolutely.

"Oh, leave Ben here for the little time you'll be with us. I'll vouch for him."

Mellowed already by pleasant anticipations, Mason Tyler allowed himself to be persuaded, and setting the two negroes who accompanied him to watch Ben, he went away to the big house.

It was perhaps two hours later when a negro groom was sent to bed Tyler's horse for the night, while one of his own servants was dispatched to tell his family that he could not be home that night.

Ben, perfectly confident that he was to "die for an old sheep," was making the best of his time, even while expecting every moment to be called to go home for punishment. But when the news of his master's determination to stay reached him, his fears faded, and he prepared to enjoy himself until fatigue stopped him. As for Hannah, she was joyous even though, woman-like, she could not shut her eyes to the doubtful future.

It was near twelve o'clock on the crisp, bright, Christmas morning that followed when Mason Tyler called for his horse to ride home. He was mellow and jovial and the red in his face was less apoplectic. He called for his horse, but he did not call for Ben, for during the night and morning Fullerton had gained several promises from him; one that he would not whip the runaway, the other, that Ben might spend the week.

Ash-Cake Hannah and Her Ben

One will promise anything to one's host, especially when that host's cellar is the most famous in six counties.

It was with joyous hearts that Ash-Cake— now Happy—Hannah and Ben watched the departure of Tyler. When he was gone, Ben whooped and cut the pigeon-wing, while Hannah, now that the danger was past, uttered a reproving: "You is de beatenes'! I mos' wish he'd 'a tuk you erlong now;" and turned to open her Christmas presents.

DIZZY-HEADED DICK.

Those were troublous times on the plantation, both for master and for man. The master only should have been concerned; but nothing ever went on at the "big house" that "the quarters" did not feel and know. And they had good reason to know this. The master had been specially irritable that morning, and Dinah told Aunt Fannie that he had driven Jim, the valet, from the room, and had shaved himself—an unprecedented happening, for Bradley Fairfax had never before been known to refuse the delicate attentions of his favorite serving-man.

There was another reason, too, why the quarters should know all about the trouble, for was not Dinah herself the weathervane whose gyrations in the quarters had only to be watched to know which way the wind blew at the big house, and when Big Ben from the Norton plantation came over to visit her Emily, as he had been doing for a year past, had she not driven him from the place?

"I ain't a-raisin' darters," she said indignantly, "to th'ow away on de likes o' dem No'ton niggahs; w'en Em'ly m'ay, I spec' huh to look fu' biggah game in tallah trees."

"But, Dinah," said Aunt Fannie, "yo' been lettin' Ben gallant Em'ly right erlong fu' mos' nigh a yeah; huccome yo' done change so quick?"

Dinah turned upon her interlocutor the look of disgust which is only possible with a match-making matron as she replied: "La, A'nt Fannie, chile, you don' know? I let huh go 'long o' him case I hadn't 'skivered yit dat de niggah had any 'tentions. Soon ez I did, I made him faihly fly."

Aunt Fannie laughed significantly, because she knew her people so well, and said with apparent irrelevance: "I ain't seed Mas' Tawm No'ton up to de big house fu' a day er so."

It was irrelevant, but confidential.

"Heish, honey; Mas' Bradley done driv' him away too long 'go to talk 'bout. He 'lows how ef Mis' Marg'et cain't find no bettah match fu' huhse'f dan Tawm No'ton she kin des' be a ol' maid, lak huh A'nt Marg'et."

"Whut's de mattah wid Mas' Tawm? He good quality an' mighty well off?"

"Whut's de mattah? W'y, he wil' ez a young deeh; whut wid hoss-racin' an' gwine down de ribber to Noo O'leans, he des' taihin' up awful Jack!"

"But hol' on; I don' see de rights o' dat. Ol' Phœbe say dat Mas' hisse'f was one o' de hoss-racin'est, travelin'-erroun'est young mans in de country w'en he was a-comin' erlong."

"Sh-sh; maybe he done been dat, but den Mas' he settled down."

"Den w'y don' he give Mas' Tawm a chanst? A hoss got to be a colt fus', ain't he?"

"Look hyeah, A'nt Fannie, whut's de mattah'd you? I don't keer ef a hoss uz got to be a colt fus'; nobody ain't gwine to buy no colt w'en he want a ca'ige hoss."

"No, indeedy, an' yo' cain't tell me! No ca'ige hoss ain't gwine to 'mount to nuffin' 'less'n he been a purty lively colt."

"Go 'long, A'nt Fannie!"

"Clah out, Dinah!"

Aunt Fannie was wiser than she seemed. She was the cook for the big house, and from the vantage ground of her kitchen, which sat just a little way off the back veranda, she saw many things. Besides, her son Dick was a house boy, and he told her others.

Dizzy-Headed Dick

She and Dick had special reasons for loving and cherishing the young Miss Margaret, for, when angry at some misdemeanor of the black boy's, Bradley Fairfax had threatened to sell him down the river, it had been the young woman's prayers rather than Aunt Fannie's wailings that had turned him from his determination. So they worshiped her, and Dick would have died for her.

On the day that the storm rose to its height Dick slipped down to his mother's kitchen with the news.

"Whut's de mattah'd you, Dick?" asked his mother.

"Sh, mammy, but dey's goin's on up dah."

"Wha kin' o' gwine on, huh?"

"I hyeahd Mas' Bradley talkin' to young Mis' dis mo'nin', an' I tell you fu' a little w'ile it was mannahs."

"Whut'd he say to my little lammy?"

"Dey was talkin' 'bout Mas' Tawm No'ton, an' she tol' him dat Mas' Tawm wasn't so wil' ez he used to be, an' he uz a-settlin' down. Mas' he up an' said dat Tawm No'ton didn't come o' a settlin-down fambly, an' dey wouldn't be no weddin' in his house 'tween huh an' a No'ton.

Den she ax him ef he an' Mas' Tawm's pa wa'n't great frien's w'en dey was young, an' he say, c'ose; but dey had come to de pa'tin' o' de ways long befo' ol' man Tawm No'ton died.

"Mis' Marg'et, she 'plied up, 'Well, fathah, I hope you won't fo'ce yo' darter to steal away lak a thief in de night to ma'y de man she loves.' "

" 'I ain't 'fraid,' ol' Mas' says; 'no Fairfax lady have evah done dat.' 'Den watch th'oo de day,' she answeh back, an' den I didn't hyeah no mo'. It 'pears lak to me Mas' Bradley ain't so sot ag'in Mas' Tawm No'ton, case he come out purty soon an' kicked Jim, an' w'en he right mad he don't ac' dat a-way. Seem lak he des' kin' o' whimsy an' stubbo'n; but it's goin' to mek somep'n happen."

"How yo' know whut it gwine to do?"

" 'Case I saw Mis' Marg'et ride down to de big gate, an' w'en she thought nobody was lookin' tek a lettah out o' de post, an' w'en she rode back huh lips was a-set in de Fairfax way, so I'm gwine to keep my eye peeled th'oo de day."

"Oomph, is dat all you know?"

"Yes'm."

"Well, you clah out, you black rascal; you been eavesdrappin' ag'in, dat's whut you been doin'. You ought to be ashamed o' yo'se'f. Don' you come hyeah a'tellin' me no mo' o' yo' eavesdrappin' trash; clah out!"

"Yes'm, I'm a-goin', but you keep yo' eahs open, mammy, an' yo' eyes, too; an' mammy, 'membah hit's ouah Mis' Marg'et!"

"Clah out, I tell you!" and Dick went his way. "Ouah Mis' Marg'et; sic himpidence!" mused the old woman as she began to beat the dough for the biscuits; "ouah Mis' Marg'et—my po' little lamb!"

If Tom Norton had only known it, he had two strong allies in any designs he might have.

Aunt Fannie affected to ignore Dick's injunctions. Nevertheless, in the ensuing days she followed his advice and kept her eyes open. They were so wide open and so busy with diverse things that on two mornings she sent in burned biscuits to the big house, and was like to lose her reputation.

However, all waiting must sometime end, and Aunt Fannie's watchfulness was rewarded when she saw one morning a carriage and pair dash up the front drive, circle the house, and halt at the back veranda.

"I couldn't mek out whut was de mattah," she afterward told Dinah, "w'en I seed dat ca'ige flyin' roun' de house widout stoppin'; den all of a suddint I seed my lammy come a'runnin' out wid a mantilly ovah huh haid, an' I look at de ca'ige ag'in, an' lo an' behol'; dah stood young Mas' Tawm No'ton, hol'in' out his ahms to huh. She runned right past de kitchen, an' whut you think dat blessed chile do? She stop an' fling huh ahms roun' my ol' naik an' kiss me, an' hit's de livin trufe, I'd 'a' died fu' huh right dah. She wa'n't no mo' den ha'f way to de ca'ige w'en ol' Mas' come des' a-ragin' an' a-sto'min' to de do', an' Lawd, chile, 'fo' I knowed it I was a-hollerin', 'Run, baby, run!' She did run, too, an' Mas' Tawm he run to meet huh and tuk huh by de han.'

"Den I seed my Dick runnin', too, an' I hyeahed Mas' Bradley hollah: 'Cut de traces, Dick; cut de traces!' I stepped back an' reached fu' my meat cleavah. Ef dat boy'd 'a' teched dem traces I's mighty 'feahed I'd 'a' th'owed it at him an' cut ouah 'lationship in two, but I see Mis' Marg'et tu'n an' look back ovah huh shoul-

der at him des' as she step in de ca'ige. She gin
him a kin' o' 'pealin look, but hit a 'fidin' look,
too, an' all of a suddint dat rascal's han's went
up in de aih an' he fell flat on de grass. Ol'
Mas' kept a'screamin' to him to cut de traces,
but c'ose, 'fo' he could git up de hosses was a-
sailin' down de road, an' Mis' Marg'et was
a'wavin' huh han' kin' o' sad lak outen de ca'ige
windah; but la' Mas' Tawm gin one look at
Dick a-layin' dah in de grass an' faihly split his
sides wid laffin.' De las' I seed o' dem ez dey
made de tu'n he was still a'hol'in' hisse'f.

"Well, Mas' Bradley he come a sto'min' down
an' kick Dick. 'Git up,' he say, 'git up, you black
scoun'el,' an' Dick raise his haid kin' o' weak lak,
an' say 'Huh?' Well, I lak to died; I didn't
know de boy had so much dev'ment in him.

"Ol Mas' he grab him an' yank him up, an'
he say: 'W'yn't you cut dem traces?' An' Dick
he look up an' 'ply, des' ez innercent: 'W'y,
Mas' Bradley, I was tuk wid sich a dizz'ness in
my haid all o' de sudden hit seemed lak I was
tu.'nin' roun' and roun'.'

" 'I give you dizz'ness in yo' haid,' ol' Mas'
hollah; 'tek him up on de po'ch an' tie him to
one o' dem pillahs!' So Bob an' Jim tuk him

up an' tied him to one o' de pillahs, an' ol' Mas'
went inter de house."

Here Dinah broke in: "I was in dah w'en he
comed. Me an' ol' Mis' had des' got back f'om
town, an' Mas' Bradley he say, 'Well, a fellah
dat'll drive right up in a man's ya'd an' tek his
darter f'om under his nose mus' have some'p'n
in him,' an' ol' Mis' she laff an' cry altogethah.
I spec' she uz in de secret. I ain' so down on
Big Ben ez I was."

"La, Dinah, you is de beatenes'—— But
wait; lemme tell you——"

"Don' I know de res'?"

"You don't know 'bout de coffee?"

"No; whut 'bout de coffee?"

"Aftah w'ile Mas' Bradley sent a whole string
o' little darkies down to my kitchen an' mek me
give each of 'em a cup o' coffee; den he ma'ched
'em all in line up to Dick an' mek him drink all
de coffee.

" 'Whut you want me drink all dis coffee fu'?'
Dick say, an' Mas' Bradley he look mighty
se'ious an' 'ply: 'I's tryin' to cuoah dat dizzy
haid o' yo'n.' Well, suh, I wish't yo'd 'a'
hyeahed dem little rascallions. Dey des' rolled
on de grass an' hollahed, 'Dizzy-haided Dick!

Dizzy-Headed Dick

Dizzy-haided Dick!' an' Mas' he tu'ned an' went
in de house. I reckon dat name'll stick to de boy
'twell he die; but I don't keer, he didn't go back
on his young Mis', dizzy haid er no dizzy haid,
an' Mas' Bradley he gwine fu'give de young
folks anyhow. Ef he ain't, huccome he didn't
taih Dick all to pieces?"

THE CONJURING CONTEST.

The whole plantation was shocked when it became generally known that Bob, who had been going with Viney for more than a year, and for half that time had publicly escorted her to and from meeting, had suddenly changed, and bestowed his affections upon another. It was the more surprising, for Viney was a particularly good-looking girl, while the new flame, Cassie, was an ill-favored woman lately brought over from another of the Mordaunt plantations.

It was one balmy Sunday evening that they strolled up from the quarters' yard together, arm in arm, and set wagging the tongues of all their fellow-servants.

Bob's mother, who was sitting out in front of her door, gave a sigh as her son passed with his ungainly sweetheart. She was still watching them with an unhappy look in her eyes when Mam' Henry, the plantation oracle, approached and took a seat on the step beside her.

"Howdy, Mam' Henry," said Maria.

"Howdy, Maria; how you come on?"

"Oh, right peart in my body, but I'm kin' o' 'sturbed in my min'."

"Huh, I reckon you is 'sturbed in yo' min'!" said the old woman keenly. "Maria, you sholy is one blin' 'ooman."

"Blin'? I don't know whut you mean, Mam' Henry; how's I blin'?"

"You's blin', I tell you. Now, whut you s'pose de mattah wid yo' Bob?"

"De mattah wid him? Dat des' whut trouble my min'. Mam' Henry, hit's to think dat dat boy o' mine 'u'd be so thickle-minded!"

"Uh!"

"Hyeah he was a-gwine 'long o' Viney, whut sholy is a lakly gal, an' a peart one, too; den all o' a sudden he done change his min', an' tek up wid dat ol' ha'd-time lookin' gal. I don' know whut he t'inkin' 'bout."

"You don' know whut he t'inkin' 'bout? Co'se you don' know whut he t'inkin' 'bout, an' I don' know whar yo' eyes is, dat you can't see somep'n' dat's des' ez plain ez de nose on yo' face."

"Well, I 'low I mus' be blin', Mam' Henry, 'ca'se I don' understan' it."

"Whut you reckon a lakly boy lak Bob see on dat gallus niggah?"

"I don' know, Mam' Henry, but dey do say she bake mighty fine biscuits, an' you know Bob's min' moughty close to his stomach."

"Biscuits, biscuits," snorted the old woman; " 'tain't no biscuits got dat man crazy. Hit's roots, I tell you; hit's roots!"

"Mam' Henry, fo' de Lawd, you don' mean—"

The old woman leaned solemnly over to her companion and whispered dramatically: "He's conju'ed; dat's whut he is!"

Maria sprang up from the doorway and stood gazing at Mam' Henry like a startled animal; then she said in a hurried voice: "Whut! dat huzzy conju' my chile? I—I—I'll kill huh; dat's whut I will."

"Yes, you kill huh, co'se you will. I reckon dat'll tek de spell offen Bob, won't hit? Dat'll kep him f'om hatin' you, an' des pinin' erway an' dyin' fu' huh, won't hit, uh?"

Maria sank down again in utter helplessness, crying: "Conju'ed, conju'ed; oh, whut shell I do?"

"Fus' t'ing," said Mam' Henry, "you des set up an' ac' sensible. Aftah dat I'll talk to you."

The Conjuring Contest

"Go on, Mam' Henry; I's a-listenin' to you.
Conju'ed, conju'ed, my boy! Oh, de—"

"Heish up, an' listen to me. Befo' Bob put
on his shoes termorrer mornin' you slip a piece o'
silvah in de right one, flat in de middle, whah he
won' feel it. You want to fin' out how he's conju'ed, an' des' how bad it is. Ef she ain't done
nuffin' but planted somep'n' roun' de do' fu' him,
why I reckon des' sowin' salt'll brek de spell; but
ef she's cotch him in his eatin's you'll have to see
a reg'lar conju' doctah fo' you kin wo'k dat out.
I ain't long-haided myse'l; but I got a frien' dat
is."

"But, Mam' Henry, how I gwine tell how bad
de conju' is?"

"Huh, gal, you don' know nuffin'! Ef de
silvah tu'ns right black, w'y, he's cotched bad,
an' ef it only tu'ns kin' o' green he's only middlin' tricked."

"How long I got to wait 'fo' I knows?"

"Let him wah de silvah th'ee er fo' days, an'
den let me see it."

Maria did as she was told, placing a dime in
the bottom of her son's shoe, and at the expira-
tion of the alloted time, with eyes fear and
wonder wide, she took the coin to her instructor.

Whether from working in the field all day the soil had ground into Bob's shoe and discolored the coin, or whether it had attracted some subtle poison from the wearer's body, is not here to be decided. From some cause the silver piece was as dark as copper.

Mam' Henry shook her head over it. "He sho' is cotched bad," she said. "I reckon she done cotched him in his eatin's; dat de wuss kin'. You tek dat silvah piece an' th'ow it in de runnin' watah."

Maria hesitated; this was part of a store she was saving for a particular purpose.

"W'y does I has to do dat, Mam' Henry?" she asked. "Ain' dey no othah way?"

"Go 'long, gal; whut's de mattah wid you? You do ez I tell you. Don' you know dat any- t'ing you buy wid dat money'd be bad luck to you? Dat ah dime's chuck full o' goophah, clah to de rim."

So, trembling with fear, Maria hastened to the branch and threw the condemned coin into it, and she positively asserted to Mam' Henry on her return that the water had turned right black and thick where the coin sunk.

"Now, de nex' t'ing fu' you to do is to go down an' see my frien', de conju' doctah. He live down at de fo'ks o' de road, des' back o' de ol' terbaccer house. Hit's a skeery place, but you go dah ter-night, an' tell him I sont you, an' he lif' de spell. But don' you go down dah offerin' to pay him nuffin', 'ca'se dat 'stroy his cha'ms. Aftah de wo'k done, den you gin him whut you want, an' ef it ain't enough he put de spell back on ergin. But mustn' nevah ax a conju' doctah whut he chawge, er pay him 'fo' de cha'm wo'k, no mo'n you mus' say thanky fu' flowah seed."

About nine that night, Maria, frightened and trembling, presented herself at the "conju' doc-tah's" door. The hut itself was a grewsome looking place, dark and dilapidated. The yard surrounding it was overrun with a dense growth of rank weeds which gave forth a sickening smell as Maria's feet pressed them. The front window was shuttered, and the sagging roof sloped down to it, like the hat of a drunken man over a bruised eye.

The mew of a cat, the shuffling of feet and a rattle of glass followed the black woman's knock, and Maria pictured the terrible being within hastening to put away some of his terrible decoctions before admitting her. She was so afraid that she had decided to turn and flee, leaving Bob to his fate, when the door opened and the doctor stood before her.

He was a little, wizened old man, his wrinkled face the color of parchment. The sides of his head were covered with a bush of gray hair, while the top was bald and blotched with brown and yellow spots. A black cat was at his side, looking with evil eyes at the visitor.

"Is you de conju' doctah?" asked Maria.

He stepped back that she might enter, and closed the door behind her. "I's Doctah Bass," he replied.

"I come to see you—I come to see you 'bout my son. Mam' Henry, she sont me."

"Well, le' m' hyeah all erbout it." His manner was reassuring, if his looks were not, and somewhat encouraged, Maria began to pour forth the story of her woes into the conjure doctor's attentive ear. When she was done he sat for a while in silence, then he said:

"I reckon she's got some o' his ha'r—dat meks a moughty strong spell in a 'ooman's han's. You go back an' bring me some o' de' 'ooman's ha'r, an' I fix it, I fix it."

136

The Conjuring Contest

"But how's I gwine git any o' huh ha'r?"

"Dat ain' fu' me to say; I des' tell you whut to do."

Maria backed out of the bottle-filled, root-hung room, and flew home through the night, with a thousand terrors pressing hard upon her heels.

All next day she wondered how she could get some of her enemy's hair. Not until evening did the solution of the problem come to her, and she smiled at its simplicity. When Cassie, her son's unwelcome sweetheart, came along, she stepped out from her cabin door and addressed her in terms that could mean but one thing—fight. Cassie attacked Maria tooth and nail, but Maria was a wiry little woman, and when Bob separated the two a little later his mother was bruised but triumphant, for in her hand she held a generous bunch of Cassie's hair.

"You foun' out a way to git de ha'r," said the conjure doctor to her that night, "an' you ain't spaihed no time a-gittin' it."

He was busy compounding a mixture which looked to Maria very much like salt and ashes. To this he added a brown thing which looked like the dried liver of some bird. Then he put in a portion of Cassie's hair. The whole of this he wrapped up in a snake's skin and put in a bag.

"Dat'll fetch him," he said, handing the bag to Maria. "You tek dis an' put it undah his baid whah he won' fin' it, an' sprinkle de res' o' dis ha'r on de blanket he lay on, an' let hit stay dah seven days. Aftah dat he come roun' all right. Den you kin come to see me," he added significantly.

Clasping her treasure, Maria hastened home and placed the conjure bag under her son's bed, and sprinkled the short, stiff hair as she had been directed. He came in late that night, hurried out of his clothes and leaped into bed. Usually he went at once to sleep, but not so now. He rolled and tossed, and it was far past midnight before his regular breathing signified to the listening mother that he was asleep. Then with a murmured, "De conju' is a-wokin' him," she turned over and addressed herself to rest.

The next morning Bob was tired and careworn, and when asked what was the matter, responded that his dreams had been troubled. He was so tired when the day's work was over that he decided not to go and see Cassie that night.

"'DAT'LL FETCH HIM,' HE SAID, HANDING THE BAG TO MARIA'"

He was just about going to bed when a tap came at the cabin door, and Viney came in.

"Evenin', A'nt Maria," she said; "evenin', Bob."

"Evenin'," they both said.

"I des' run in, A'nt Maria, to bring you some o' my biscuits. Mam' Henry done gi' me a new 'ceipt fu' mekin' dem." She uncovered the crisp, brown rolls, and the odor of them reached Bob's nose. His eyes bulged, and he paused with his hand on his boot.

"La," said Maria, "dese sho' is nice, Viney. He'p yo'se'f, Bob."

Bob suddenly changed his mind about going to bed, and he and Viney sat and chatted while the biscuits disappeared. Maria discreetly retired, and she said to herself as she sat outside on the step: "Dey ain't no way fu' dat boy to 'sist dat goophah an' dem biscuits, too."

Bob's dreams were troubled again that night, and the next, and as the evenings came he still found himself too tired to go a-courting. All this was not lost on the watchful mother, and she duly reported matters to Mam' Henry, who transferred her information to Cassie in the following manner:

"Hit sholy don' seem right, Sis' Cassie, w'en Bob gwine 'long o' you, fu' him to be settin' up evah night 'long o' dat gal Viney."

And Cassie, who was a high-spirited girl, replied:

"Uh, let de niggah go 'long; I don' keer nuffin' 'bout him."

Next time she met Bob she passed without speaking to him, and, strange to say, he laughed, and didn't seem to care, for Mam' Henry's biscuit receipt had made Viney dearer to him than she had ever been. Up until the eighth night his dreams continued to be troubled, but on that night he slept easily, and dreamed of Viney, for Maria had removed the conjure bag and had thrown it into running water. What is more, she had shaken the hair out of the blanket.

The first evening that Bob felt sufficiently rested to go out skylarking it was with Viney he walked, and the quarters nodded and wondered. They walked up to the master's house, where the momentous question was asked and favorably answered. Then they came back radiant, and Viney set out some biscuits and preserves in her cabin to clinch it, and invited Maria and Mam' Henry to share them with Bob and her.

The Conjuring Contest

That night sundry things from the big house, as well as lesser things from Maria's cabin found their way to the "conju' doctah's." The things from the big house were honestly procured, but it took the telling of the whole story by Maria to get them.

When she had gone, her master, Dudley Stone, laughed to himself, and said with true Saxon incredulity: "That old rascal, Bass, is a sharp one. I think lying on Cassie's hair would trouble anybody's dreams, conjure or no conjure, and if Viney learned to make biscuits like Mammy Henry she needed no stronger charm."

DANDY JIM'S CONJURE SCARE.

Dandy Jim was very much disturbed when he came in that morning to shave his master. He was Dandy Jim, because being just his master's size, he came in for the spruce garments which Henry Desmond cast off. The dark-skinned valet took great pride in his personal appearance, and was little less elegant than the white man himself. He was such a dapper black boy, and always so light and agile on his feet that his master looked up in genuine surprise when he came in this morning looking care-worn and dejected, and walking with a decided limp.

To the question, "Why, what on earth is the matter with you, Jim?" he answered only with a doleful shake of his head.

"Why, you look like you'd been getting religion."

"No, I ain't quite as bad as dat, Mas' Henry. Religion 'fects de soul, but hits my body dats 'fected."

"You've been getting your feet wet, I reckon, and it's cold."

"I wish 'twas; I wish 'twas," said Jim sadly.

"You wish it was? Well, what is the matter with you?"

"Mas' Henry, kin you let me have a silver dime? I's been hurted."

"Jim!"

"I tell you I's been tricked."

"And you believe in that sort of thing after all I've tried to teach you?"

"Mas' Henry, I tell you, I's been tricked. Dey ain't no 'sputin' de signs, teachin' er no teachin'!"

"Well, I wish you'd tell me the signs so that I'd know them. It's just possible that I may have been tricked some time and didn't know it."

"Don' joke, Mas' Henry, don' joke. Dis is a se'ious mattah, an' 'f you'd 'a' evah been tricked an' hit done right, you'd 'a' knowed, case dey 'ain't no 'sputin' de symptoms. Dey's mighty well known. W'en a body's tricked, dey's tricked, an' dat's de gospel truf."

"Do you claim to know them?"

"Don' I tell you I's a sufferin' f'om dem now?"

"Well, what are they?"

"Well, fu' one t'ing, I's got a mighty mis'ry in my back, an' I got de limb trimbles, an' I's des' creepy all ovah in spots, dat's a sho' sign, whenevah you feels spotted. I tells you, Mas' Henry, somebody's done laid fu' me an' cotch me. I wish you'd please, suh, gimme a piece o' silvah to lay on de place."

"What will that do?"

"W'y, I wants to be right sho', fo' I goes to a conju' doctah, an' ef I is tricked, de silvah, hit'll show it, 'dout a doubt. Hit'll tu'n right black."

"Jim," said the white man, as he handed over the silver coin, "I've never known you to talk this way before, and I believe you've got some oher reason for believing you're conjured besides the ones you've given me. You rascal, you've been up to something."

The valet grinned sheepishly, hung his head and shuffled his feet in a way that instantly confessed judgment.

"Come, own up now," pressed his master, "what devilment have you been up to?"

"I don' see how it's any dev'ment fu' a body to go to see de gal he like."

'Uh-huh, you've been after somebody else's girl, have you? And he's fixed you, eh?"

144

"I didn't know 'Lize was goin' 'long o' anybody else 'twell I went in thaih de othah night
to see huh, an' even den, she nevah let on nuffin'.
We talked erlong, an' laughed, an' was havin' a
mighty fine time. You see 'Lize, she got a
powahful drawin' way erbout huh. I kep' on
settin' up nighah an' nighah to huh, an' she kep'
laughin', but she nevah hitched huh cheer away,
so co'se I thought hit was all right, an' dey wa'nt
nobody else a-keepin' comp'ny wid huh. W'en,
lo, an' behol', des' as I was erbout to put my ahm
erroun' huh wais', who should walk in de do' but
one dem gret big, red-eyed fiel'-han's. Co'se I
drawed erway, fu' dat man sho' did look dang'-
ous. Well, co'se, a gent'man got to show his
mannahs, so I ups an' says, "Good-evenin', suh,'
an' meks my 'bejunce. Oomph, dat man nevah
answered no mo'n I'd been a knot on a log, an'
him anothah. Den 'Lize she up an say, 'Good-
evenin', Sam, an' bless yo' soul, ef he didn't treat
huh de same way. He des' went ovah in de
cornder an' sot down an' thaih he sot, a-lookin'
at us wid dem big red eyes o' his'n a-fai'ly
blazin'! Well, I seed dat 'Lize was a-gittin'
oneasy, an' co'se, hit ain't nevah perlite to be a

inconwenience to a lady, so I gits up an' takes my hat, an' takes my departer."

"The fact, in other words, is, you ran from the man."

"No, suh, a pusson couldn't 'zactly say I run. I did come erway kind o' fas', but you see, I was thinkin' 'bout 'Lize's feelin's an' hit seemed lak ef I'd git out o' de way, it'd relieve de strain."

"Yes, your action does great credit to your goodness of heart and your respect for your personal safety, Jim."

Jim flashed a quick glance up into his master's face. He did not like to be laughed at, but his eyes met nothing but the most serious of expressions, so he went on: "Dat uz two nights ago, an' evah sence den, I been feelin' mighty funny. I des' mo'n 'low dat Sam done laid fu'me, an' cotch me in de back an' laig. You know, Mas' Henry, dem ah red-eyed people, dey mighty dang'ous, an' it don' do nobody no good to go 'long a-foolin' wid 'em. Ef I'd 'a' knowed dat Sam was a-goin' 'long o' 'Lize, I sholy would 'a' fed 'em bofe wid a long spoon. I do' want nobody plantin' t'ings fu' me."

"Jim, you're hopeless. Here I've tried my best to get that conjuring notion out of your head. You've been brought up right here in the house with me for three or four years, and now the first thing that happens, you fall right back to those old beliefs that would be unworthy of your African grandfather."

"Mas' Henry, I ain' goin' to 'spute none o' yo' teachin's, an' I ain' goin' to argy wid you, 'case you my mastah, an' it wouldn' be perlite, but I des' got one t'ing to say, dat piece o' silvah you gi' me, 'll tell de tale."

The valet now having finished his work and his complaints, went his way, leaving his master a bit disgusted, and a good deal amused. "These great overgrown children," he mused, "still frightened by fairy tales."

It was late in the afternoon before the master saw his servant again. Then he opened his eyes in astonishment at him.

Henry Desmond was sitting on the porch, when the black man hove in sight. He would have slipped round to the back of the house and entered that way had not his master called to him. Dandy Jim, a dandy no longer, approached and stood before his speechless owner. He was

147

a figure for gods and men to behold. He was covered with dirt from head to foot. His clothes looked as though he might have changed raiment with an impoverished scarecrow. One sleeve was gone out of his coat, and the leg of his trousers was ripped from the knee down. A half a dozen scratches and bruises disfigured his face, and when he walked, it was with a limp more decidedly genuine than the one of the morning. But the feature that utterly surprised Henry Desmond, that took away his speech for a moment or two, was the beautiful smile that sat on Jim's countenance.

The master finally found his voice, "Jim, what on earth is the matter? You look like a storm had struck you."

"Oh, Mas' Henry, I ain' conjuahed, I ain' conjuahed!"

"You ain't conjured? Well, you look a good deal more like you'd been conjured than you did this morning. I should take it for granted that a whole convention of witches and hoodoos had sat on your case."

"No suh, no suh, I ain' conjuahed a-tall."

"Well, what's the matter with you, then?"

"W'y, suh, I's seed dat red-eyed fiel-han' Sam, an' he pu't nigh walloped de life out o' me, yes, suh, he did."

"Well, you take it blessed cheerful."

"Dat's becase I knows I ain' conjuahed."

"Didn't the silver turn black? You know it might not have had time yet!"

"Mas' Henry, I ain' bothahed nuffin' 'bout de silvah, I ain' 'pendin' on dat. De reason I knows I ain' conjuahed, Sam, he done whupped me. I was a goin' down to de fiel' 'long 'bout dinnah time, an' who should I meet but Sam. 'Hol' on, Jim,' he say, a settin' down de bucket he was ca'in' to de fiel'. 'Hol' on,' he say, an' I stop 'twell he come up. 'Jim,' he say, 'you was down in the quahtahs a-settin' up to Miss 'Lize night befo' last', wasn't you?' 'Well, I was present,' say I, 'on dat occasion, w'en I had de pleasure o' meetin' you.' 'Nemmine dat, nemmine dat,' he say,' 'I do' want none o' yo' fine wo'ds what you lu'n up to de big house, an' uses crookid down in de quahtahs;' but bless yo' soul, Mas' Henry, dat wa'nt true—'I do' want none o' yo' fine wo'ds;' den he tuk off his hat, an' rolled up his sleeves—he sholy has got awful ahms. 'I's goin' to whup you,' says he, an', well, suh, he did. He

149

whupped me mos' scan'lous. He des' walloped me all ovah de groun'. Oomph, I nevah shell fu'git it! W'y, dat man lak to wo' me out. Seemed lak, w'en he fust sta'ted, he was des' goin' to give me a little dressin' down, but he seemed to waken to de wo'k ez he pu'sued his co'se. W'en he got thoo, he say, 'Now ef evah I ketches you foolin' 'roun' Miss 'Lize agin, I'll brek you all ter pieces.' Den I come away rejoicin' 'case I knowed I wa'nt tricked."

"Well, you're the first man I ever saw rejoice over such a thrashing as you've had. What do you mean? How do you know you're not conjured?"

"W'y, Mas' Henry, what's de use o' conjuahin' a man w'en you can whup him lak dat? Hain't dat enough satisfaction? Dey ain't no need to go 'roun' wo'kin wid roots w'en you got sich fistes ez Sam got."

"But you had so much confidence in the silver this morning. What does the silver say?"

"La, Mas' Henry, aftah Sam whupped me dat 'way I was so satisfied in my min' dat I des' tuk off de silvah an bought lin'ment wid it. You kin cuoah bruises wid lin'ment, an' you allus knows des how to reach de case, but conjuah, dat's diff'unt." And Jim limped away to apply his lotion to his sore, but unconjured body.

THE MEMORY OF MARTHA.

You may talk about banjo-playing if you will, but unless you heard old Ben in his palmy days you have no idea what genius can do with five strings stretched over the sheepskin.

You have been told, perhaps, that the banjo is not an expressive instrument. Well, in the hands of the ordinary player it is not. But you should have heard old Ben, as bending low over the neck, with closed eyes, he made the shell respond like a living soul to his every mood. It sang, it laughed, it sighed; and, just as the tears began welling up into the listener's eyes, it would break out into a merry reel that would set one's feet a-twinkling before one knew it.

Ben and his music were the delight of the whole plantation, white and black, master and man, and in the evening when he sat before his cabin door, picking out tune after tune, hymn, ballad or breakdown, he was always sure of an audience. Sometimes it was a group of white children from the big house, with a row of pickaninnies pressing close to them. Sometimes it was old Mas' and Mis' themselves who strolled up to the old man, drawn by his strains. Often there was company, and then Ben would be asked to leave his door and play on the veranda of the big house. Later on he would come back to Martha laden with his rewards, and swelled with the praise of his powers.

And Martha would say to him, "You, Ben, don' you git conceity now; you des' keep yo' haid level. I des' mo'n 'low you been up dah playin' some o' dem ongodly chunes, lak Hoe Co'n an' Dig 'Taters."

Ben would laugh and say, ,"Well, den, I tek de wickedness offen de banjo. Swing in, ol' 'ooman!" And he would drop into the accompaniment of one of the hymns that were the joy of Martha's religious soul, and she would sing with him until, with a flourish and a thump, he brought the music to an end.

Next to his banjo, Ben loved Martha, and next to Ben, Martha loved the banjo. In a time and a region where frequent changes of partners were common, these two servants were noted for their single-hearted devotion to each other. He had never had any other wife, and she had called no other man husband. Their children had grown up and gone to other plantations, or to cabins of their own. So, alone, drawn closer by the habit of comradeship, they had grown old together—Ben, Martha and the banjo.

One day Martha was taken sick, and Ben came home to find her moaning with pain, but dragging about trying to get his supper. With loud pretended upbraidings he bundled her into bed, got his own supper, and then ran to his master with the news.

"Marfy she down sick, Mas' Tawm," he said, "an' I's mighty oneasy in my min' 'bout huh. Seem lak she don' look right to me outen huh eyes."

"I'll send the doctor right down, Ben," said his master. "I don't reckon it's anything very serious. I wish you would come up to the house to-night with your banjo. Mr. Lewis is going to be here with his daughter, and I want them to hear you play."

It was thoughtlessness on the master's part; that was all. He did not believe that Martha could be very ill; but he would have reconsidered his demand if he could have seen on Ben's face the look of pain which the darkness hid.

"You'll send de doctah right away, Mas'?"

"Oh, yes; I'll send him down. Don't forget to come up."

"I won't fu'git," said Ben as he turned away. But he did not pick up his banjo to go to the big house until the plantation doctor had come and given Martha something to ease her. Then he said: "I's got to go up to de big house, Marfy; I be back putty soon."

"Don' you hu'y thoo on my 'count. You go 'long, an' gin Mas' Tawm good measure, you hyeah?"

"Quit yo' bossin," said Ben, a little more cheerfully; "I got you whah you cain't move, an' ef you give me any o' yo' back talk I 'low I frail you monst'ous."

Martha chuckled a "go 'long," and Ben went lingeringly out of the door, the banjo in its ragged cover under his arm.

The plantation's boasted musician played badly that night. Colonel Tom Curtis wondered what was the matter with him, and Mr. Lewis told his daughter as he drove away that it seemed as if the Colonel's famous banjoist had been overrated. But who could play reels and jigs with the proper swing when before his eyes was the picture of a smoky cabin room, and on the bed in it a sick wife, the wife of forty years?

The black man hurried back to his cabin where Martha was dozing. She awoke at his step.

"Didn't I tell you not to hu'y back hyeah?" she asked.

"I ain't nevah hu'ied. I reckon I gin 'em all de music dey wanted," Ben answered a little sheepishly. He knew that he had not exactly covered himself with glory. "How's you feelin'?" he added.

" 'Bout de same. I got kin' of a mis'ry in my side."

"I reckon you couldn't jine in de hymn to tek de wickedness outen dis ol' banjo?" He looked anxiously at her.

"I don' know 'bout j'inin' in, but you go 'long an' play anyhow. Ef I feel lak journeyin' wid you I fin' you somewhar on de road."

The banjo began to sing, and when the hymn was half through Martha's voice, not so strong and full as usual, but trembling with a new pathos, joined in and went on to the end. Then Ben put up the banjo and went to his rest.

The next day Martha was no better, and the same the next. Her mistress came down to see her, and delegated one of the other servants to be with her through the day and to get Ben's meals. The old man himself was her close attendant in the evenings, and he waited on her with the tenderness of a woman. He varied his duties as nurse by playing to her, sometimes some lively, cheerful bit, but more often the hymns she loved but was now too weak to follow.

It gave him an aching pleasure at his heart to see how she hung on his music. It seemed to have become her very life. He would play for no one else now, and the little space before his door held his audience of white and black children no more. They still came, but the cabin door was inhospitably shut, and they went away whispering among themselves, "Aunt Martha's, sick."

Little Liz, who was a very wise pickaninny, once added, "Yes, Aunt Marfy's sick, an' my mammy says she ain' never gwine to git up no mo'." Another child had echoed "Never!" in the hushed, awe-struck tones which children use in the presence of the great mystery.

Liz's mother was right. Ben's Martha was never to get up again. One night during a pause in his playing she whispered, "Play 'Ha'k! F'om de Tomb.'" He turned into the hymn, and her voice, quavering and weak, joined in. Ben started, for she had not tried to sing for so long. He wondered if it wasn't a token. In the midst of the hymn she stopped, but he played on to the end of the verse. Then he got up and looked at her.

Her eyes were closed, and there was a smile on her face—a smile that Ben knew was not of earth. He called her, but she did not answer. He put his hand upon her head, but she lay very still, and then he knelt and buried his head in the bedclothes, giving himself up to all the tragic violence of an old man's grief.

"Marfy! Marfy! Marfy!" he called. "What you want to leave me fu'? Marfy, wait; I ain't gwine be long."

His cries aroused the quarters, and the neighbors came flocking in. Ben was hustled out of the way, the news carried to the big house, and preparations made for the burying.

Ben took his banjo. He looked at it fondly, patted it, and, placing it in its covering, put it on the highest shelf in the cabin.

"'MARFY!' HE CALLED. 'WHAT YOU WANT TO
LEAVE ME FU'?'"

"Brothah Ben allus was a mos' p'opah an' 'sponsible so't o' man," said Liz's mother as she saw him do it. "Now, dat's what I call showin' 'spec' to Sis Marfy, puttin' his banjo up in de ve'y place whah it'll get all dus'. Brothah Ben sho is diff'ent f'om any husban' I evah had." She had just provided Liz with a third step-father.

On many evenings after Martha had been laid away, the children, seeing Ben come and sit outside his cabin door, would gather around, waiting, and hoping that the banjo would be brought out, but they were always doomed to disappointment. On the high shelf the old banjo still reposed, gathering dust.

Finally one of the youngsters, bolder than the rest, spoke: "Ain't you gwine play no mo', Uncle Ben?" and received a sad shake of the head in reply, and a laconic "Nope."

This remark Liz dutifully reported to her mother. "No, o' co'se not," said that wise woman with emphasis; "o' co'se Brothah Ben ain' gwine play no mo'; not right now, leas'ways; an' don' you go dah pesterin' him, nuther, Liz. You be perlite an' 'spectable to him, an' make yo' 'bejunce when you pass."

The child's wise mother had just dispensed with her latest stepfather.

The children were not the only ones who attempted to draw old Ben back to his music. Even his master had a word of protest. "I tell you, Ben, we miss your banjo," he said. "I wish you would come up and play for us sometime."

"I'd lak to, Mastah, I'd lak to; but evah time I think erbout playin' I kin des see huh up dah an' hyeah de kin' o' music she's a-listenin' to, an' I ain't got no haht fu' dat ol' banjo no mo'."

The old man looked up at his master so pitifully that he desisted.

"Oh, never mind," he said, "if you feel that way about it."

As soon as it became known that the master wanted to hear the old banjo again, every negro on the plantation was urging the old man to play in order to say that his persuasion had given the master pleasure. None, though, went to the old man's cabin with such confidence of success as did Mary, the mother of Liz.

"O' co'se, he wa'n't gwine play den," she said as she adjusted a ribbon; "he was a mo'nin'; but now—hit's diffe'nt," and she smiled back at herself in the piece of broken mirror.

She sighed very tactfully as she settled herself on old Ben's doorstep.

"I nevah come 'long hyeah," she said "widout thinkin' 'bout Sis Marfy. Me an' huh was gret frien's, an' a moughty good frien' she was."

Ben shook his head affirmatively. Mary smoothed her ribbons and continued:

"I ust to often come an' set in my do' w'en you'd be a-playin' to huh. I was des' sayin' to myse'f de othah day how I would lak to hyeah dat ol' banjo ag'in." She paused. " 'Pears lak Sis Marfy 'd be right nigh."

Ben said nothing. She leaned over until her warm brown cheek touched his knee. "Won't you play fu' me, Brothah Ben?" she asked pleadingly. "Des' to bring back de membry o' Sis Marfy?"

The old man turned two angry eyes upon her. "I don' need to play," he said, 'an' I ain' gwineter. Sis Marfy's membry's hyeah," and tapping his breast he walked into his cabin, leaving Mary to take her leave as best she could.

It was several months after this that a number of young people came from the North to visit the young master, Robert Curtis. It was on the second evening of their stay that young Eldridge said, "Look here, Colonel Curtis, my father visited your plantation years ago, and he told me of a wonderful banjoist you had, and said if I ever came here to be sure to hear him if he was alive. Is he?"

"You mean old Ben? Yes, he's still living, but the death of his wife rather sent him daft, and he hasn't played for several years."

"Pshaw, I'm sorry. We laughed at father's enthusiasm over him, because we thought he overrated his powers."

"I reckon not. He was truly wonderful."

"Don't you think you can stir him up?"

"Oh, do, Col. Curtis," chorused a number of voices.

"Well, I don't know," said the Colonel, "but come with me and I'll try."

The young people took their way to the cabin, where old Ben occupied his accustomed place before the door.

"Uncle Ben," said the master, "here are some friends of mine from the North who are anxious to hear you play, and I knew you'd break your rule for me."

"Chile, honey——" began the old man.

But Robert, his young master, interrupted him. "I'm not going to let you say no," and he hurried past Uncle Ben into the cabin. He came out, brushing the banjo and saying, "Whew, the dust!"

The old man sat dazed as the instrument was thrust into his hand. He looked pitifully into the faces about him, but they were all expectancy. Then his fingers wandered to the neck, and he tuned the old banjo. Then he began to play. He seemed inspired. His listeners stood transfixed.

From piece to piece he glided, pouring out the music in a silver stream. His old fingers seemed to have forgotten their stiffness as they flew over the familiar strings. For nearly an hour he played and then abruptly stopped. The applause was generous and real, but the old man only smiled sadly, and with a far-away look in his eyes.

As they turned away, somewhat awed by his manner, they heard him begin to play softly an old hymn. It was "Hark! From the Tomb."

He stopped when but half through, and Robert returned to ask him to finish, but his head had fallen forward close against the banjo's neck, and there was a smile on his face, as if he had suddenly had a sweet memory of Martha.

WHO STAND FOR THE GODS.

There was a warm flush of anger on Robert Curtis' face as he ran down the steps of the old Stuart mansion. Every one said of this young man that he possessed in a marked degree the high temper for which his family was noted. And one looking at him that night would have said that this temper had been roused to the utmost.

This was not the first time Robert Curtis had ridden away from the Stuarts' in anger. Emily Stuart was a high-strung girl, independent, and impatient of control, and their disagreements had been many. But they had never gone so far as this one, and they had somehow always blown over. This time the young lover had carried away in his pocket the ring with which they had plighted their troth, and had gone away vowing never to darken those doors again, and Emily had been exasperatingly polite and cool, though her eyes were flashing as she assured him how little she ever wanted to look upon his face again.

It may have been the strain of keeping this self-possession that made her break down so completely as soon as her lover was out of sight. That she did break down is beyond dispute, for when Dely came in with a very much disordered waistband she found her mistress in tears.

With the quick sympathy and easy familiarity of a favorite servant she ran to her mistress exclaiming, "La, Miss Em'ly, whut's de mattah?"

Her Miss Emily waved her away silently, and drying her eyes stood up dramatically.

"Dely," she said, "Mr. Curtis will not come here any more after to-day. Certain things have made it impossible. I know that you and Ike are interested in each other, and I do not want the changed relations between Mr. Curtis and me to make any difference to you and Ike."

"La, Miss Em'ly," said Dely, surreptitiously straightening her waistband, "I don' keer nuffin' 'bout Ike; he ain't nuffin' 'tall to me."

"Don't fib, Dely," said Emily impressively.

" 'Claih to goodness, Miss Em'ly, I ain't fibbin'; but even if Ike was anyt'ing to me you know I wa'n't nevah 'spectin' to go ovah to the Cu'tis plantatin 'ceptin' wid you, w'en you an' Mas' Bob——"

"That will do, Dely." Emliy caught up her handkerchief and hurried from the room.

"Po' Miss Em'ly," soliloquized Dely; "she des natchully breakin' huh hea't now, but she ain't gwine let on. Ike, indeed! I ain't bothahed 'bout Ike," and then she added, smiling softly, "That scamp's des de same ez a b'ah; he mighty nigh ruined my ap'on at de wais'."

Robert Curtis was crossing the footbridge which separated the Curtis and Stuart farther fields before Ike rode up abreast of him. The bay mare was covered with dust and foam, and a heavy scowl lay darkly on the young man's face.

Finding his horse blown by her hard gallop, the white man drew rein, and they rode along more slowly, but in silence. Not a word was spoken until they alighted, and the master tossed the reins to his servant.

"Well," he said bitterly, "when you go to the Stuarts' again, Ike, you'll have to go alone."

"Then I won't go," said Ike promptly.

"Oh, yes, you will; you're fool enough to be hanging around a woman's skirts, too; you'll go."

"Whaih you don' go, I don' go."

"Well, I don't go to the Stuarts' any more, that's one thing certain." Robert was very young.

"Then I don' go," returned Ike doggedly; "don' you reckon I got some fambly feelin's?"

The young man's quick anger was melting in its own heat, and he laughed in spite of himself as he replied: "Neither family feelings nor anything else count for much when there's a woman in the case."

"Now, I des wonder," said Ike, as he led the horses away and turned them over to a stable boy, "I des wonder how long this hyeah thing's goin' on? De las' time they fell out fu' evah hit was fou' whole days befo' he give in. I reckon this time it might run to be a week."

He might have gone on deluding himself thus if he had not suddenly awakened to the fact that more than the week he had set as the limit of the estrangement had passed and he had not yet been commanded to saddle a horse and ride over to the Stuarts' with the note that invariably brought reconciliation and happiness.

He felt disturbed in his mind, and his trouble visibly increased when, on the next day, which was Sunday, Quin, who was his rival in everything, dressed himself with more than ordinary care and took his way toward the Stuarts'.

"Whut's de mattah wid you, Ike?" asked one of the house boys next day; "you goin' to let Quin cut you out? He was ovah to Stua'ts' yistiddy, an' he say he had a ta'in' down time wid Miss Dely."

"Oh, I don' reckon anybody's goin' to cut me out."

"Bettah not be so sho," said the boy; "bettah look out."

This was too much for Ike. He had been wavering; now his determination gave way, yet he tried to delude himself.

"Hit's a shame," he said. "I des know Mas' Bob is bre'kin' his hea't to git back to Miss Em'ly, an' hit do seem lak somep'n 'oughter be done to gin him a chancet."

It needed only the visit from his master that afternoon to decide him. He was out on the back veranda cleaning shoes, when his master came and stood in front of him, flicking his boots with his riding-whip.

"Ah, Ike, you haven't been over to Mr. Stuart's lately."

"No, suh; co'se not; I ain't been ovah."

"Well, I don't believe I'd do that, Ike. Don't let my affair keep you away; you go on and see her. You don't know; she might be sick or something, and want to see you. Here's fifty cents; take her something nice." And with the very erroneous idea that he had fooled both Ike and himself, Robert Curtis went down the steps whistling.

"What'd I tell you?" said Ike, addressing the shoe which sat upon his hand, and he began to hurry.

Dely was sitting on the doorstep of her mother's cabin as Ike came up. She pretended not to see him, but she was dressed as if she expected his coming.

"Howdy, Dely; how you this evenin'?" said Ike.

"La, Mistah Ike," said Dely, affecting to be startled, "I come mighty nigh not seein' you. Won't you walk in?"

"No, I des tek a seat on de do'step hyeah 'longside you."

She tossed her head, but made room for him on the step.

"I ain't seen you fu' sev'al days."

"You wasn' blin' ner lame."

"No, but you know," answered Ike rather doggedly.

"I don' know nuffin'," Dely returned.

"I wasn' 'spected to come alone."

"Was you skeered?"

"Did you want me to come alone?"

Dely did not deign to answer.

"I wonder how long this is goin' on?" pursued Ike; "I'm gittin' mighty tiahed of it."

"They ain't no tellin'. Miss Em'ly she mighty high-strung."

"Well, hit's a shame, fu' them two loves one another, an' they ought to be brought togethah."

"Co'se they ought; but how anybody goin' to do it?"

"You an' me could try ef you was willin'."

"I'd do anything fu' my Miss Em'ly."

"An' I'd do anything fu' Mas' Bob. Come an' le's walk down by de big gate an' talk about it."

Dely rose, and together they walked down by the big gate, where they stood in long and earnest conversation. Maybe it was all about their master's and mistress' love affair. But a soft breeze was blowing, and the moon was shining in the way which tempts young people to consider their own hearts, however much they may be interested in the hearts of others.

It was some such interest which ostensibly prompted Robert Curtis to sit up for Ike that night. Ike came into the yard whistling. His master was sitting on the porch.

"Ike, you are happy; you must have had a good time."

Instantly Ike's whistle was cut short, and the late moonlight shone upon a very lugubrious countenance as he answered:

"Sometimes people whistles to drown dey sorrers."

"Why, what sorrows have you got? Wasn't Dely in a pleasant mood?"

"Dely's mighty 'sturbed 'bout huh Miss Em'ly."

"About her Miss Emily!" exclaimed the young master in sudden excitement; "what's the matter with Miss Emily?"

"Oh, Dely says she des seems to be a-pinin' 'bout somep'n'. She don' eat an' she don' sleep."

"Poor litt——" began Curtis, then he checked himself. "Hum," he said. "Well, good-night, Ike."

When Ike had gone in, his master went to his room and paced the floor for a long while. Then he went out again and walked up and down the lawn. "Maybe I'm not treating her just right," he murmured; "poor little thing, but ——" and he clenched his fist and kept up his walking.

"Ike was here to-night?" said Miss Emily to Dely as the maid was brushing her hair that night.

"Yes'm, he was hyeah."

"Yes, I saw him come up the walk early, and I didn't call you because I knew you'd want to talk to him," she sighed.

"Yes'm, he wanted to talk mighty bad. He feelin' mighty 'sturbed 'bout his Mas' Bob."

The long, brown braid was quickly snatched out of her hand as her young mistress whirled swiftly round.

"What's the matter with his master?"

"Oh, Ike say he des seem to pine. He don' seem to eat, an' he don' sleep."

Miss Emily had a sudden fit of dreaming from which she awoke to say, "That will do, Dely; I won't need you any more to-night." Then she put out her light and leaned out of her window, looking with misty eyes at the stars. And something she saw up there in the bright heavens made her smile and sigh again.

Who Stand for the Gods

It was on the morrow that Dely told her mistress about some wonderful wild flowers that were growing in the west woods in a certain nook, and Dely was so much in earnest about it that her mistress finally consented to follow her thither.

Strange to say, that same morning Ike accosted his young master with, "Look hyeah, Mas' Bob, de birds is sholy thick ovah yondah in that stretch o' beechwoods. I've polished up the guns fu' you, ef you want to tek a shot."

"Well, I don't mind, Ike. We'll go for a while."

It was in this way—quite by accident, of course, one looking for strange flowers, and the other for birds—that Emily and Robert, with their faithful attendants, set out for the same stretch of woods.

Miss Emily was quite despairing of ever finding the wonderful flowers, and Ike was just protesting that he himself had "seen them birds," when all of a sudden Dely exclaimed: "Well, la! Ef thaih ain't Mas' Cu'tis."

Miss Emily turned pale and red by turns as Robert, blushing like a girl, approached her, hat in hand.

"Miss Emily."

"Mr. Curtis."

Then they both turned to look for their attendants. Ike and Dely were walking up a side path together. They both broke into a laugh that would not be checked.

"It would be a shame to disturb them," Robert went on when he could control himself. "Emily, I've been a——"

"Oh, Robert!"

"Let us take the good that the gods provide."

"And they," said Emily, looking after the blacks, "stand for the gods."

A LADY SLIPPER.

On that particular night in June it pleased Miss Emily Stuart to be gracious to Nelson Spencer. Robert Curtis was away, attending court at the county seat, and really, when one is young and beautiful and a woman, it is absolutely necessary that there should be some person upon whom to try one's charms. So the lady was gracious to her ardent, but oft-rejected lover. She was sitting on the step of the high veranda and he a little below her. Her tiny foot, shod in the daintiest of slippers, swung dangerously near him. She knew that he was looking admiringly at the glimpse of pointed toe which now and then he got from beneath her skirt, and it pleased her. She was rather proud of that pretty, aristocratic foot of hers, not so much because it was pretty and aristocratic as because it was hereditary in the family and belonged by right of birth to all the Stuarts.

It was a warm, soft night, a night just suited for love and dreams. The sky like a blue-black cup inverted, seemed pouring a shower of gems upon the earth, and the breeze was laden with the sweet smell of honeysuckle and the heavier odor of magnolia blossoms.

They were not talking much because it wasn't worth while. After an extended period of silence he looked up at her and sighed, perhaps because he wanted to, maybe because he couldn't help it.

"What are you sighing for?" she asked.

"Oh, just at the beauty of things."

"Why, that should make you smile."

"Not always. If there is sometimes a grief too deep for tears, there is at others a joy too great for smiles."

"You ought to have been a poet, Nelson, you are so sentimen——"

"Spare me that."

"No I shall not. You are sentimental to the last degree."

"Oh, well, I may be; if it is sentimentality to be willing to grovel in the dirt for a lady's slipper, then I am sentimental." Emily Stuart laughed.

"You know you would look very ridiculous groveling in the dirt. Would you really do it for my slipper?"

"Yes."

"I'll put you to the test, then; you shall have my slipper when I see you grovel."

He hesitated. "What," she laughed, "am I too literal?"

"No," he said; "I mean what I say," and he leaped from the porch to the road beyond and fell upon his knees in the dust of the carriage-way.

The spectacle amused Emily, and disgusted her no little. A woman pretends that she wants a man to abase himself before her, but she never forgives him if he does. While he knelt there in the road she thought how differently Robert would have acted under the circumstances. Instead of groveling, he would probably have said, "I'll be hanged if I do," and she rather liked the thought of his saying that. She knew that so far as brains went, Robert could not compare with Nelson; she knew, too, that the wisest man has the greatest capacity for making a fool of himself.

After an interval, Nelson arose from his position and came back to the veranda.

"I claim my reward," he said.

"Do you think you can rightly call that groveling?"

"Yes, without a doubt."

"Then you shall not go unrewarded," and, turning, she went into the house to return with a slipper, a dainty little beribboned thing, which she handed to him. She was quite used to his extravagant protestations, and only thought to put a light significance upon his words. She was unprepared, then, to see him put the slipper into his pocket as if he really meant to keep it.

The evening passed away, and though they talked much, no reference was made to the slipper until he rose to go. Then Emily said, "Has your desire for my slipper been sufficiently satisfied?"

"Oh, no," he replied, "I shall keep this as the outward sign and the reward of my abasement."

"You are really not going to keep it?"

"Oh, but I am. You gave it to me."

"I did not mean it in that way."

"The sight of me groveling there in the road I gave you to remember for all time, and the gift that I ask in return is a permanent one."

"And it is of no use for me to argue with you?"

"None."

"Nor plead?"

"No."

"Very well," said Emily with a vain effort at calmness, "I wish you joy of your treasure. Good-night," and she went into the house. But she watched him from behind the curtain until he was quite gone; then she came flying out again and made her way hastily toward the quarters whither she knew her maid Dely had gone to spend the evening. When she had brought her to the big house, she exclaimed breathlessly:

"Oh, Dely, Dely, I am in such trouble!"

"Do tell we what is de mattah now."

"Oh, Nelson Spencer has been here and——"

"Miss Em'ly," Dely broke in, "you been ca'in on wid dat man agin?"

"Why, Dely, how can you say such things? Carrying on, indeed! I was only trying to put him in his place by making him ridiculous, but I gave him my slipper, and he—he kept it."

"He got yo' slippah? Miss Em'ly, don' tell me dat."

"Oh, what shall I do, Dely, what shall I do? Suppose Robert should go there and see it on his bureau or somewhere—you know they are such friends—what would he say? He'd be bound to recognize it, you know. They're the

179

ones with the silver buckles and satin bows that he liked so well. One could never explain to Robert; he's so impetuous. Dely, don't stand there that way. You must help me."

"What shell I do, Miss Em'ly? I reckon you'd bettah go an' have yo' pa frail dat slippah outen him."

"What? Papa? Why, I wouldn't have him to know anything about it for the world."

"Why, it ain't yo' fault, Miss Em'ly; you in de rights of de thing."

"Oh, yes, yes, I know, but a thing like that is so hard to explain. Dely, you must get that slipper."

"How I'm goin' to?"

"I don't know; you'll have to find some way. You'll find some way to get it before Robert comes. You will, won't you, Dely?"

"When do Mas' Robert come?"

"He'll surely be home in a couple of days."

"An he's mighty cu'ious, ain't he?"

"If he should happen to come across that slipper in Nelson Spencer's room, all would be over between us. Oh, Dely, you must find some way."

"Mas' Nelson Spencah is right sma't boas'ful, ain't he?"

"Oh, Dely."

"You don't reckon he'd show it to Mas' Robert, do you?"

"Dely, you're saying everything to frighten me; don't talk that way."

"Miss Em'ly, de truth is de light; but nevah min', I'll try an' git dat slippah fu' you."

"Oh, Dely, and you shall have that blue sprigged muslin dress of mine you liked so much."

Dely's eyes gleamed but she answered, "Nevah you min' about de dress, Miss Em'ly. What we wants is de slippah," and the maid departed to think.

For a long while she thought of everything she knew, and canvassed every resource within her power. Of course, she might make love to Harry, Spencer's valet, and have him get the prize for her, but then she knew that Ike would be sure to find that out and get angry with her. She might appeal to Carrie, one of the Spencer household, but she knew that Carrie hated her and would do anything rather than gratify her slightest wish, for Carrie herself had an eye on Ike.

Then might she not steal it herself? But how to effect an entrance to the room of her mistress' enemy?

"Lawd bless me," she exclaimed suddenly, her eyes brightening, "I done fu'git young Mas' Roger. I spec he'll be snoopin' roun' some place to-morrer."

Now Dely knew that Nelson Spencer had a brother, a reckless, disobedient boy, who had just arrived at the unspeakable age. Something in this knowledge or rather in the sudden recollection, sent her flying to the kitchen, where for something over two hours she braved Aunt Hester's maledictions while she baked heap upon heap of crisp sweet cakes.

When, hot and tired, she had finished and placed them in a cloth-covered jar, she chuckled to herself with the remark, "Now, ef dat don't fetch dat slippah, I reckon Miss Em'ly bettah look out fu' anothah gallant; but I know dat boy."

On the following morning, the maid, carrying a bulging bag, wandered out in the direction of the Spencer place, hoping to meet young Roger somewhere in the open air, on his pony or nosing about the woods on foot. She had said that she knew that boy, and she did. Roger was a boy with a precocious appetite. He might be backward in everything else, but his ability to consume food was large beyond his years. He lived to eat. He went into the house to browse, and came out of it to forage. He was insatiable. When kitchen and orchard had done their part in vain, he had recourse to roots of the field and strange, unaccountable plants which would have proved his death but for the intervention of that Providence which is popularly supposed to take care of three certain irresponsible classes of humanity.

Dely was not mistaken in thinking he would be "snooping about" somewhere, for it was not long before she saw him walking along the road munching an apple and looking for more food. She hastened to catch up with him, and, like a sensible girl, approached him from the windward side.

"Howdy, Roger?" said Dely invitingly.

"Hullo, Dely."

"Whaih you goin'?"

"I don' know; where are you goin'?" eyeing the bag. Dely must have put ginger into those sweet cakes and Roger's scent was keen.

"Oh, I'm jest walkin' erroun'."

"What you got in your bag?"

"Now jest listen at dat chile," exclaimed Dely with a well-feigned surprise and admiration. "Now who'd a thought you'd tek notice o' dis hyeah ol' bag. Nev' you min' what I got in dis bag."

"Seems like I smell somethin' good."

"Don' bothah me, Roger; I ain't got no time to fool wid you. Seems to me lak you always want to be eatin' some'p'n."

"Then it is eatin', Dely?"

"Who said so? Dat's what I want to know; who said so?"

"Why, you did, you did, that's who," Roger cried gleefully.

"Did I? Well, la sakes! Who'd 'a' evah thought o' me givin' myself away dat away? I mus' be gittin' right rattle-brained. I don' b'lieve I said it."

"Oh, yes, you did. Let's see, Dely. Do let's see."

"Oh, I dassent," said the dissembler. "Hit's some'p'n fine."

Roger fairly danced with excitement. "Do, do," he pleaded; "just one little peep."

"I'm feared you'll want to eat some."

"Oh, no, I won't. Please let me look?"

Dely carefully opened the mouth of the bag and slowly inclined it toward the eager boy. Even before the brown beauty of the cakes broke on the boy's sight the fragrant odor of them had reached his nostrils. Then he saw them. Just one flash of russet and gold and the maid closed the bag with a jerk, but not before she was aware that she had a willing slave at her feet.

"Oh, Dely!" the boy gasped.

"Well, I mus' be gittin' 'long now."

"Dely, just one. Oh, Dely!"

"Now what'd I tell you? Didn't I say you'd be wantin' one? I cain't stop to bothah wid you. Dese is luck cakes."

" Luck cakes?" Roger's curiosity for the moment almost overcame his hunger. "What's luck cakes? "

Miss Emily's diplomat took one of them from the bag.

"You see dis hyeah cake," she said, holding it dangerously near Roger's nose, while his hands twitched, "you see dis hyeah cake. Well, ef you go out of a mornin' wid a bag of dese an' ef anybody can bring you a unmatched slippah befo' dey's all et up, you has luck fu' de rest o' yo' life, an' de pusson what brings de slippah gits de rest o' de cakes."

"Gets them all, Dely?" asked Roger faintly.

"All dat's lef'."

"Ain't you eatin' yourself, Dely?"

"No, I ain't 'lowed to eat 'em. It'll spile de chawm."

Just then Dely let the golden cake drop in his hand. When the last crumb had disappeared he asked, "Dely, what's an unmatched slipper?"

"Why, it's one dat ain't got no mate, of cou'se. Jest a one-footed slippah."

"Oh, I can get you one."

"You! De ve'y ideeh!"

"Yes, I can, too; mamma has lots of odd ones."

"No, no," said Dely hastily, "you musn't git yo' mammy's. No 'ndeedy. Dat 'u'd spile de chawm."

"Charms are funny things, ain't they?" said the boy.

"Mighty funny, mighty funny. You nevah know whaih dey goin' to break out. But 'bout dis chawm," and she handed him another cake, "you musn't git de slippah of no lady what belongs to you, ner of no man, ner you musn't let nobody know dat you teken' it, fu' dat 'u'd break de chawm, too. De bes' way is to go in yo' brothah Nelson's room an' look erroun' right sha'p, an' mebbe you might fin' a little weenchy slippah wid ribbons er some'p'n on it, an' dat'll be de luck slippah."

"Oh," exclaimed Roger, "I know there couldn't be such a slipper in brother Nelson's room."

Dely paused dramatically and closed her bag. "Well, I got to be goin'," she said. "I mus' fin' somebody else to bring me de luck slippah."

"I'll go, Dely, I'll go," cried Roger, starting; "but Dely, promise you won't let anybody else eat those cakes. It might spoil the charm."

"Well, I'll give you anothah one, jes' fu' strengf," and she laughed a laugh of triumph as the boy sped away.

"I 'low ef dey's any slippah thaih he'll fin' it, 'long ez he smell dese hyeah cakes in his min'."

Dely had not long to wait for her courier. Pretty soon he came bounding toward her waving something in his hand. He was radiant.

"I found it, Dely, I found it, just as you said. It was on the bureau. Now I may have the cakes, mayn't I?"

"It's de luck slippah, thank goodness,," said Dely solemnly as she eagerly clutched the missing piece of foot-wear.

"Now I may have the cakes, mayn't I?" Roger was dancing again.

"Yes, ef you'll promise you'll never, never tell," said Dely, "so's 't'll not break de chawm."

"Hope m' die, Dely."

Then she poured the cakes on the ground beside him, and, leaving him to his joy, went home laughing to her mistress.

"How *did* you get it, Dely?" asked her mistress, clasping her accusing shoe.

"Oh, I wo'ked my chawms," Dely replied.

Miss Emily was walking along the road that evening with thoughtful eyes cast on the ground. She knew that Nelson Spencer was behind her.

"What are you looking for?" he asked as he overtook her.

"A flower," she said.

"A flower! What particular one?"

"A lady-slipper."

"Aren't you a little far south for it?" His house was to the north.

"I think I have found it," she said, facing him and planting both feet firmly within sight.

" 'I THINK I HAVE FOUND IT,' SHE SAID "

A Lady Slipper

Spencer looked down, and, bowing low, passed on, but she could see the flush that started in his brow, spreading from cheek to neck, and she laughed cheerily.

Nelson Spencer went home to say unrepeatable things to his valet, the butler, the housekeeper and Carrie the maid, in fact, to everybody except Roger, who was, at the time, suffering the pangs of precocious indigestion.

A BLESSED DECEIT.

As Martha said, "it warn't long o' any sma't-ness dat de rapscallion evah showed, but des 'long o' his bein' borned 'bout de same time ez young mastah dat Lucius got tuk into de big house." But Martha's word is hardly to be taken, for she had a mighty likely little picka-ninny of her own who was overlooked when the Daniels were looking about for a companion for the little toddler, their one child. Martha might have been envious. However, it is true that Lu-cius was born about the same time that his young Master Robert was, and it is just possible that that might have had something to do with his appointment, although he was as smart and likely a little darkey as ever cracked his heels on a Vir-ginia plantation. Years after, people wondered why that black boy with the scarred face and hands so often rode in the Daniels' carriage, did so little work, and was better dressed than most white men. But the story was not told them; it touched too tender a spot in the hearts of all who knew. But memory deals gently with old

190

wounds, and the balm of time softens the keenest sorrow.

Lucius first came to the notice of Mr. Daniels when as a two-year-old pickaninny he was rolling and tumbling in the sand about the quarters. Even then, he could sing so well, and was such a cheerful and good-natured, bright little scamp that his master stood and watched him in delight. Then he asked Susan how old he was, and she answered, "La, Mas' Stone, Lucius he 'bout two years old now, don't you ricollec'? He born 'bout de same time dat little Mas' Robert came to you-alls." The master's eyes sparkled, and he tapped the black baby on the head. His caress was immediately responded to by a caper of enjoyment on the youngster's part. Stone Daniels laughed aloud, and said, "Wash him, Susan, and I'll send something down from the house by Lou, then dress him, and send him on up." He turned away, and Susan, her heart bounding with joy, seized the baby in her arms and covered his round black body with kisses. This was a very easy matter for her to do, for he only wore one pitiful shift, and that was in a sadly dilapidated condition. She hurried to fulfil her master's orders.

There was no telling what great glory might come of such a command. It was a most wonderful blue dress with a pink sash that Lou brought down from the house, and when young Lucius was arrayed therein, he was a sight to make any fond mother's heart proud. Of course, Lucius was rather a deep brunette to wear such dainty colors, but plantation tastes are not very scrupulous, and then the baby Robert, whose garments these had been, was fair, with the brown hair of the Daniels, and was dressed accordingly.

Half an hour after the child had gone to the big house, Susan received word that he had been appointed to the high position of companion in chief, and amuser in general to his young master, and the cup of her earthly joy was full. One hour later, the pickaninny and his master were rolling together on the grass, throwing stones with the vigorous gusto of two years, and the sad marksmanship of the same age, and the blue dress and pink sash were of the earth, earthy.

"I tell you, Eliza," said Stone, "I think I've struck just about the right thing in that little rascal. He'll take the best care of Robert, and I think that playing like that out in the sunshine will make our little one stronger and healthier. Why, he loves him already. Look at that out there." Mrs Daniels did look. The young scion of the Daniels house was sitting down in the sand and gravel of the drive, and his companion and care taker was piling leaves, gravel, dirt, sticks, and whatever he could find about the lawn on his shoulders and head. The mother shuddered.

"But don't you think, Stone, that that's a little rough for Robert, and his clothes—oh my, I do believe he is jamming that stick down his throat!"

"Bosh," said Stone, "that's the way to make a man out of him."

When the two children were brought in from their play, young Robert showed that he had been taken care of. He was scratched, he was bruised, but he was flushed and happy, and Stone Daniels was in triumph.

One, two, three years the companionship between the two went on, and the love between them grew. The little black was never allowed to forget that he was his Master Robert's servant, but there is a democracy about childhood that oversteps all conventions, and lays low all barriers of caste. Down in the quarters, with many secret giggles, the two were dubbed, "The Daniels twins."

It was on the occasion of Robert's sixth birthday that the pair might have been seen "codgin'" under the lilac bush, their heads very close together, the same intent look on both the black and the white face. Something momentous was under discussion. The fact of it was, young Master Robert was to be given his first party that evening, and though a great many children of the surrounding gentry had been invited, provision had not been made for the entertainment of Lucius in the parlor. Now this did not meet with Robert's views of what was either right or proper, so he had determined to take matters in his own hands, and together with his black confederate was planning an amendment of the affair.

"You see, Lucius," he was saying, "you are mine, because papa said so, and you was born the same time I was, so don't you see that when I have a birthday party, it is your birthday party too, and you ought to be there?"

"Co'se," said Lucius, with a wise shake of the head, and a very old look, "Co'se, dat des de way it look to me, Mas' Robert."

"Well, now, as it's your party, it 'pears like to me that you ought to be there, and not be foolin' 'round with the servants that the other company bring."

"Pears lak to me dat I oughter be 'roun' dah somewhah," answered the black boy.

Robert thought for awhile, then he clapped his little knee and cried, "I've got it, Lucius, I've got it!" His face beamed with joy, the two heads went closer together, and with many giggles and capers of amusement, their secret was disclosed, and the young master trotted off to the house, while Lucius rolled over and over with delight.

A little while afterwards Robert had a very sage and professional conversation with his father in the latter's library. It was only on state occasions that he went to Doshy and asked her to obtain an interview for him in that august place, and Stone Daniels knew that something great was to be said when the request came to him. It was immediately granted, for he denied his only heir nothing, and the young man came in with the air and mien of an ambassador bearing messages to a potentate.

What was said in that conversation, and what was answered by the father, it boots not here to tell. It is sufficient to say that Robert Daniels came away from the interview with shining eyes and a look of triumph on his face, and the news he told to his fellow conspirator sent him off into wild peals of pleasure. Quite as eagerly as his son had gone out to Lucius, Stone Daniels went to talk with his wife.

"I tell you, Eliza," he said, "there's no use talking, that boy of ours is a Daniels through and through. He is an aristocrat to his finger tips. What do you suppose he has been in to ask me?"

"I have no idea, Stone," said his wife, "what new and original thing this wonderful boy of ours has been saying now."

"You needn't laugh now, Eliza, because it is something new and original he has been saying."

"I never doubted it for an instant."

"He came to me with that wise look of his; you know it?"

"Don't I?" said the mother tenderly.

"And he said, 'Papa, don't you think as I am giving a party, an' my servant was born 'bout the same time as I was, don't you think he ought to kinder—kinder—be 'roun' where people could see him, as, what do you call it in the picture, papa?' 'What do you mean?' I said. 'Oh, you know, to set me off.' 'Oh, a background, you mean?' 'Yes, a background; now I think it would be nice if Lucius could be right there, so whenever I want to show my picture books or anything, I could just say, "Lucius, won't you bring me this, or won't you bring me that?" like you do with Scott.' 'Oh, but my son,' I said, 'a gentleman never wants to show off his possessions.' 'No, papa,' he replied, with the most quizzical expression I ever saw on a child's face, 'no, I don't want to show off. I just want to kinder indicate, don't you know, cause it's a birthday party, and that'll kinder make it stronger."

"Of course you consented?" said Mrs. Daniels.

"With such wise reasoning, how could a man do otherwise?" He replied, "Don't you see the child has glimmers of that fine feeling of social contrast, my dear?"

"I see," said Mrs. Daniels, "that my son Robert wants to have Lucius in the room at the party, and was shrewd enough to gain his father's consent."

"By the Lord!" said her husband, "but I believe you're right! Well, it's done now, and I can't go back on my word."

"The Daniels twins" were still out on the lawn dancing to the piping of the winds and throwing tufts of grass into the air and over their heads, when they were called in to be admonished and dressed. Peacock never strutted as did Lucius when, arrayed in a blue suit with shining brass buttons, he was stationed in the parlor near his master's chair. Those were the days when even children's parties were very formal and elegant affairs. There was no hurrying and scurrying then, and rough and tumble goings-on. That is, at first, there was not; when childhood gets warmed up though, it is pretty much the same in any period of the world's history. However, the young guests coming were received with great dignity and formality by their six-year-old host. The party was begun in very stately fashion. It was not until supper was announced that the stiffness and awe of the children at a social function began to wear off. Then they gathered about the table, cheerful and buoyant, charmed and dazzled by its beauty. There was a pretty canopy over the chair of the small host, and the dining-room and tables were decorated with beautiful candles in the silver candlesticks that had been heirlooms of the Daniels for centuries. Robert had lost some of his dignity, and laughed and chatted with the rest as the supper went on. The little girls were very demure, the boys were inclined to be a little boisterous. The most stately figure in the room was Lucius where he was stationed stiff and erect behind his master's chair. From the doorway, the elders looked on with enjoyment at the scene. The supper was nearly over, and the fun was fast and furious. The boys were unable longer to contain the animal spirits which were bubbling over, and there began surreptitious scufflings and nudges under the table. Someone near Robert suddenly sprang up, the cloth caught in his coat, two candles were tipped over straight into the little host's lap. The melted wax ran over him, and in a twinkle the fine frills and laces about him were a mass of flames. Instantly all was confusion, the children were shrieking and rushing pell-mell from the table. They crowded the room in frightened and confused huddles, and it was this that barred Stone Daniels as he fought his way fiercely to his son's side. But one was before him. At the

first sign of danger to his young master, Lucius
had sprung forward and thrown himself upon
him, beating, fighting, tearing, smothering, trying to kill the fire. He grabbed the delicate
linen, he tore at the collar and jacket; he was
burning himself, his clothes were on fire, but he
heeded it not. He only saw that his master was
burning, burning before him, and his boy's heart
went out in a cry, "Oh, Mas' Bob, oh, Mas'
Bob!"

Somehow, the father reached his child at last,
and threw his coat about him. The flames were
smothered, and the unconscious child carried to
his room. The children were hurried into their
wraps and to their homes, and a messenger gal-
loped away for the doctor.

And what of Lucius? When the heir of the
Daniels was in danger of his life no one had time
to think of the slave, and it was not until he was
heard moaning on the floor where he had crept
in to be by his master's bedside, that it was found
out that he also was badly burned, and a cot was
fixed for him in the same room.

When the doctor came in he shook his head
over both, and looked very grave indeed. First
Robert and then his servant was bound and

bandaged, and the same nurse attended both. When the white child returned to consciousness his mother was weeping over him, and his father with face pale and drawn stood at the foot of the bed. "Oh, my poor child, my poor child!" moaned the woman; "my only one!"

With a gasp of pain Robert turned his face toward his mother and said, "Don't you cry, mamma; if I die, I'll leave you Lucius."

It was funny afterwards to think of it, but then it only brought a fresh burst of tears from the mother's heart, and made a strange twitching about the father's mouth.

But he didn't die. Lucius' caretaking had produced in him a robust constitution, and both children fought death and gained the fight. When they were first able to sit up—and Robert was less inclined to be parted from Lucius than ever—the young master called his father into the room. Lucius' chair was wheeled near him when the little fellow began:

"Papa, I want to 'fess somethin' to you. The night of the party I didn't want Lucius in for indicatin', I wanted him to see the fun, didn't I Lucius?"

Lucius nodded painfully, and said, "Uh-huh."

"I didn't mean to 'ceive you, papa, but you know it was both of our birthdays—and—er—" Stone Daniels closed his boy's mouth with a kiss, and turned and patted the black boy's head with a tender look on his face, "For once, thank God, it was a blessed deceit."

That is why in years later, Lucius did so little work and dressed like his master's son.

THE BRIEF CURE OF AUNT FANNY.

Some people grow old gracefully, charmingly. Others, with a bitter reluctance so evident that it detracts from whatever dignity might attach to their advanced period of life. Of this latter class was Aunt Fanny. She had cooked in the Mordaunt kitchen for more years than those hands who even claimed middle-age cared to remember. But any reference to the length of time she had passed there was keenly resented by the old woman. She had been good-looking in her younger days, sprightly, and a wonderful worker, and she held to the belief in her capabilities long after the powers of her youth and middle-age were gone. She was still young when her comrades, Parker, Tempe, Doshy and Mam Henry had duly renounced their sins, got religion and confessed themselves old. She had danced beyond the time when all her comrades had grown to the stage of settled and unfrivolous Christianity. Indeed, she had kept up her gayety until she could find no men old enough to be her partners, and the young men began to ignore her; then she went into the Church. But with the cooking, it was different. Even to herself, after years had come and brought their infirmities, she would not admit her feebleness, and she felt that she had never undergone a greater trial or endured a more flagrant insult than when Maria was put into the kitchen to help her with her work. Help her with her work, indeed! Who could help her? In truth, what need had she of assistance? Was she not altogether the most famous cook in the whole county? Was she not able by herself to cope with all the duties that could possibly devolve upon her? Resentment renewed her energy, and she did her work with an angry sprightliness that belied her years. She browbeat Maria and made her duties a sinecure by doing everything just as she had done before her rival's appearance.

It was pretty hard for the younger woman, who also was active and ambitious, and there were frequent clashes between the two, but Aunt Fanny from being an autocrat had gained a consciousness of power, and was almost always victorious in these bouts. "Uh huh!" she said to Tempe, discussing the matter. "They ain't gwine to put no upstart black 'ooman oveh me, aftah all de yeahs I's been in dat kitchen. I

knows evah brick an' slat in it. It uz built fu'
me, an' I ain't gwine let nobody tek it f'om me.
No, suh, not ontwell de preacheah done tho'wed
de ashes on dis haid."

"We's all gittin' ol', dough," said Tempe
thoughtfully, "an' de young ones got to tek ouah
place."

"Gittin' ol'! gittin' ol'!" Aunt Fanny would
exclaim indignantly; "I ain't gittin' ol'. I des'
ez spry ez I was w'en I was a gal." And by
her work she made an attempt to bear out her
statement.

It would not do, though; for Time has no
illusions. Neither is he discreet, and he was telling on Aunt Fanny.

The big house, too, had felt for a long time
that she was failing, but the old master had
hesitated to speak to her, but now he felt that
she was going from bad to worse, and that something must be done. It was hard speaking to
her, but when morning after morning the breakfast was unpardonably late, the beaten biscuits
were burned and the cakes tough, it appeared
that the crisis had come. Just at this time, too,
Maria made it plain that she was not being given
her proper share of responsibility, and Stuart

Mordaunt, the old master, went down to remonstrate with Aunt Fanny.

"Now, Fanny," he said, "you know we have never complained of your cooking, and you have been serving right here in this kitchen for forty years, haven't you?"

"Yes, I has, Mas' Stua't," said Aunt Fanny, "an' I wish I could go right on fu' fo'ty yeahs mo'."

"I wish so, too, but age is telling on you just as it is on me;" he put his hand to his white head. "It is no use your working so hard any more."

"I want to work hard," said Aunt Fanny tremulously; "hit's my life."

"But you are not able to do it," said Mordaunt forcibly; "you are too old, Fanny."

She turned on him a look eager, keen and argumentative.

I's moughty sho' you older'n me, Mas' Stua't," she said.

"I know it," he said hastily. "Didn't I just say that age was telling on us both?"

"You ain't quit runnin' de plantation yit," was the calm reply.

The master was staggered for a moment, but he hurriedly rallied: "No, I haven't, but I am a good deal less active than I was twenty, ten, even five years ago. I don't work much, I only direct others—and that's just what I want you to do. Be around, direct others, and teach Maria what you know."

"It ain't in huh," sententiously.

"Put it in her; some one had to teach you."

"No, suh, I was a born cook. Nemmine, I see you want to git rid o' me; nemmine, M'ria kin have de kitchen." The old woman's voice was trembling and tears stood in her eyes, big and glistening. Mordaunt always gentle-hearted, gave in. "Well, confound it, Fanny," he broke in, "do as you please; I've nothing more to say. I suppose we'll have to go on eating your burned biscuits and tough batter-cakes as long as you please. That's all I have to say."

But with Maria there was no such easy yielding; for she knew that she had the power of the big house behind her, and in the next bout with Aunt Fanny she held her own and triumphed for the first time. The older woman's anger knew no bounds. She went sullenly to her cabin that night, and she did not rise the next morning when the horn blew. She told those who inquired that she was sick, and "I 'low," she invariably added, "dat I's either got the rheumatiz or dat black wench has conju'ed me so's to git my kitchen, 'case she knowed dat was de only way to git it."

Now Aunt Fanny well knew that to accuse one of her fellow-servants of calling in the aid of the black art was to bring about the damnation of that other servant if the story gained credence, but even she doubted that the plantation could believe anything so horrible of one so generally popular, who, besides, had her own particular following. Among the latter Mam Henry was not wont to be numbered, but she was a woman who loved to see fair play, and after having visited Aunt Fanny in her cabin, she said in secret to Aunt Tempe:

"Fanny she don't look lak no conju'ed ooman to me, an' I's gwine fin' out whether dey's anything de matter wid huh a-tall, 'case I don' b'lieve dey is. I b'lieve she's des' in one o' huh tantrums, 'case M'ria stood huh down 'bout de kitchen."

Aunt Tempe had answered: "Dey ain't no 'sputin' dat Fanny is gittin' ol' an' doty."

The Brief Cure of Aunt Fanny

The sick woman or malingerer, whichever she was, did not see the subtle motive which prompted Mam Henry's offer to nurse and doctor her. She looked upon it as an evidence of pure friendship and a tribute to her own worth on the plantation. She saw in Mam Henry, a woman older even than herself, a trusted ally in revolt against the advances of youth, and she anticipated a sympathetic listener into whose ears she might pour her confidences. As to her powers as a curer and a nurse, while Mam Henry was not actually "long-headed," she was known to be both "gifted" and "wise," and was close in the confidence of Dr. Bass, the conjure man, himself.

Although Maria went her way about the kitchen, and made the most of her new-found freedom, she heard with grief and consternation, not unmingled with a wholesome fear, the accusations which her old enemy was making against her. She trembled for what the plantation would say and do, and for what her master would think. Some of her misgivings she communicated to Aunt Tempe, who reassured her with the remark, "Nevah you min', chile, you des go 'long an' do yo' wo'k, dey's things wo'kin' fu' you in de da'k."

Meanwhile, Mam Henry had duly installed herself in her patient's cabin and entered upon her ministrations. The afflicted arm and leg were covered with greased jimson weed and swathed in bandages.

" 'Tain't no use doin' dis, Mam Henry," Aunt Fanny protested, " 'tain't a bit o' use. I's hyeah to tell you dat dis mis'ry I's sufferin' wid ain't no rheumatiz, hit's des plain conju', an' dey ain't nuffin' gwine to do no good but to meet trick wid trick."

"You lay low, chile," answered Mam Henry impressively. "I got my own idees. I's gwine to use all de rheumatiz cuohs, an' den ef you ain't no bettah, de sign will be sho' ez de wo'd dat you's been tricked. Den we gwine to use othah things."

Aunt Fanny closed her eyes and resigned herself. She could afford to wait, for she had a pretty definite idea herself what the outcome would be.

In the long hours that the old women were together it was quite natural that they should fall into confidences, and it was equally natural that Aunt Fanny should be especially interested in the doings of the kitchen and the big house. Her mistress had brought her some flannels, and good things to eat, and, while she had sympathized with her, she felt that nothing could have been more opportune than this illness that settled the question of the cooking once and forever. In one of their talks, Aunt Fanny asked her nurse what "Ol' Miss 'Liza say 'bout me bein' sick."

"She say she moughty so'y fu' you, but dat 'tain't no mo' den she 'spected anyhow, case de kitchen kin' o' open an' you gittin' too ol' to be 'roun', 'sposin' yo'se'f to all kin' o' draughts."

"Humph!" sniffed Aunt Fanny from the bed, and she flirted the rheumatic arm around in a way that should have caused her unspeakable pain. She never flinched, however.

"She don't b'lieve you conju'ed," Mam Henry went on. "She say dat's all foo'ishness; she say you des' got de rheumatiz, dat w'en you git up you gotter stay closah to yo' cabin, an' not be flyin' 'roun' whaih you tek mo' col'."

This time the rheumatic leg performed some gyrations unheard of from such a diseased member.

"Mam Henry," said Aunt Fanny solemnly, "ain't it cu'ious how little w'ite folks know 'bout natur?"

"It sho is. Ol' Mas' he say he gwine 'tiah mos' of de ol' servants, an' let 'em res' fu' de balance o' dey days, case dey been faifful, an' he think dey 'serve it. I think so, too. We been wo'kin' all ouah days, an' I know ol' Time done laid his han' heavy on my back. Ain't I right?"

"Humph!" from the bed. "Some people ages quicker'n othahs."

"Dat's de Gospel. Now wid you an' me an' Tempe an' Pahkah an' Doshy, dey ain't been nuffin quick 'bout hit, case I tell you, Fanny, chile, we's been hyeah lo dese many days."

"How M'ria git erlong?" Aunt Fanny asked uneasily.

"Oh, M'ria she des' tickled to deaf. She flyin' 'roun' same ez a chicken wid his haid wrung off. She so proud o' huhse'f dat she des cain't res', she cain't do enough. She scourin' an' she cleanin' an' she cookin' all de time, an' w'en she ain't cookin' she plannin what she gwine to cook. I hyeah ol' mas' say dat she sholy was moughty peart, an' I 'low huh battah-cakes was somep'n scrumptious. Mas' Stua't et a mess; he 'low dat ef M'ria keep on mekin' such cakes as she mek in de mornin', de m'lasses bar'l ain't gwine hol' out no time.

Aunt Fanny looked nervously toward her brogans in the corner. The camel's back was being pretty heavily laden, and a faint smile flickered over Mam Henry's shrewd face.

"You des' ought to see de aihs M'ria teks on huhse'f. She allus struttin' erroun' wid a w'ite ap'on on soon's huh wo'k's done, an' she calls huhse'f de big house cook."

This was the last straw. The camel's back went with a figurative crash. The covers were thrown back, and Aunt Fanny sprang up and seated herself on the side of the bed.

"Han' me my shoes," she said.

"W'y, Fanny, fo' de Lawd!" cried Mam Henry in well-feigned surprise. "What you gwine do?"

"I's gwine git up f'om hyeah, dat's what I's gwine do. Han' me my shoes."

"But yo' rheumatiz, yo' rheumatiz?"

"I ain't got no rheumatiz. You done cuohed me," she said, slipping into her dress as she spoke.

"But you ain't gin me de chanst to try all de cuohs yit; s'posen you tu'ns out to be conju'ed aftah all."

"Ain't ol' miss done say hit all foolishness?"

"But you done say de w'ite folks don't know nuffin 'bout natur."

"I ain't got no time to bantah wo'ds wid you, Mam Henry, I got to go to my wo'k. I ain't gwine let my kitchen be all messed up an' my w'ite folks' appetites plum spiled by dat know-nuffin wench." And Aunt Fanny walking with an ease that bore out her statement that she was cured swept out of the house with scant courtesy to her nurse, who remained behind, shaking with laughter.

"I said so, I said so," she said to herself. "I knowed dey wa'nt nuffin' de mattah wid Fanny but de tantrums."

Maria was a good deal surprised and not at all pleased when, a little later, her old rival appeared upon the scene and began to take charge of things in the old way.

"W'y, Aunt Fanny," she said, "I t'ought you was sick?"

"You don't s'pose I's gwine to stay sick all de time, do you?" was the short response. "I wants you to know I's cuohed."

Then Maria bridled. Her unlimited authority in the last few days had put added spirit into her.

"Look a-hyeah, Aunt Fanny," she said, "I sees thoo you now. You des been sick 'case you couldn't have yo' own way, an' you wanted to mek b'lieve I conju'ed you so de folks would drive me out, didn't you? But sick er no sick, conju' er no conju', cuohed er no cuohed, dis is my kitchen, an' I ain't gwine gin it up to no 'ooman."

Later on the services of the master had to be called in again, and he also began to understand.

"Well, it's this way, Fanny," he said; "you might be cured now, but if you stay around here you are likely to be taken down again. You are apt to become subject to these attacks, so you had better go back to your cabin and stay around there. Maria is going to take charge of the kitchen now, and when we need you, you can come up and cook something special for your old Miss and me."

The old woman would have protested, but there was a firm ring in her master's voice which was not to be mistaken, and she went tearfully back to her cabin, where, though so suddenly "cuohed," she was immediately taken ill again, more seriously, if possible, than before.

THE STANTON COACHMAN.

The morning sun touched the little old-fashioned Virginia church with glory, while in the shadow of its vine-covered porch an old negro alternately mumbled to himself and dozed.

It was not yet time for the service to begin, and as I stood watching the bees go in and out of the honeysuckle vines there came up the road and halted at the door a strange equipage. Side by side upon the one seat of an ox-cart sat a negro, possibly fifty years of age, and an old white lady. No one could have mistaken her for one of the country women coming in from any of the adjoining farms, for she was unmistakably a lady, from the white hair which crowned her high-bred face to the patched and shabby shoe that peeped from under her dress as she alighted. The black man had leaped down and, holding in one hand the ropes that did duty as reins, helped her tenderly to the ground.

The grace and deference of his manner were perfect, and she accepted his service with a certain genial dignity that bespoke custom. She went her feeble way into the church, and I was surprised to see the dozing old negro wake into sudden life, spring up and doff˙ his cap as she passed. Meanwhile, at the heads of the lazy oxen stood the shabby servitor, erect and fine-looking, even in the tattered garments that covered his form.

The scene would have been ludicrous if there had not been about it an air of dignified earnestness that disarmed ridicule. You could almost have imagined that black tatterdemalion there a coachman in splendid livery, standing by the side of his restless chargers, and that ox-cart with its one seat and wheels awry might have been the most dashing of victorias. What had I stumbled upon—one of those romances of the old South that still shed their light among the shadows of slavery?

The old negro in the porch had settled himself again for a nap, but I disregarded his inclination and, the service forgotten, approached him: "Howdy, Uncle."

"Howdy, son, howdy; how you come on?"

"Oh, I'm tol'able peart," I answered, falling easily into his manner of speech. "I was just wondering who the old lady was that went in church just now."

The Stanton Coachman

He looked up questioningly for a minute, and then being satisfied of my respect, replied, "Dat uz de Stanton lady—Ol' Mis' Stanton."

"And the black man there?"

"Dat's Ha'ison; dat's de Stanton coachman. I reckon you ain't f'om hyeah?"

"No, but I should like to know about them."

"Oomph, hit's a wonder you ain't nevah hyeahed tell o' de Stantons. I don' know whah yo' been at, man. Why, evahbody knowed de Stantons roun' 'bout hyeah. Dey wuz de riches' folks anywhah roun'."

"Well to do, were they?"

"Well to do! Man, whut you talkin' 'bout? I tell you, dem people wuz rich, dey wuz scand'-lous rich. Dey owned neahly all de dahkies in de county, an' dey wasn't no hi'in' out people, neithah. I didn't 'long to dem, but I allus wished I did, 'case——"

"But about Harrison?"

"Ez I were goin' to say, my ol' mastah hi'ed out, an' I wuz on de go mos' all de time, 'case I sholy wuz spry an' handy dem days. Ha'ison, he wuz de coachman, an' a proudah, finah-dressed dahky you nevah seed in all yore bo'n days. Oomph-um, but he wuz sta'chy! Dey

had his lib'ry made at de same place whah dey
made de ol' Cunnel's an' de young mastah's
clothes, an' dey wuz sights. Such gol' buttons,
an' long coats, an' shiny hats, an' boots——"
The old man paused and shook his head, as if
the final glory had been reached. "Dey ain't
no mo' times lak dat," he went on. "Hit used
to be des lak a pu'cession when Ha'ison come
ridin' down de road on top o' de Stanton ca'ige.
He sot up thar des ez straight, de hosses a
prancin', an' de wheels a glistenin', an' he
nevah move his naik to de right er de lef, no
mo'n ef he wuz froze. Sometimes you could git
a glimpse o' de mistus' face inside, an' she wuz
allus beautiful an' smilin', lak a real lady ought
to be, an' sometimes dey'd have de ca'ige open,
an' de Cunnel would come a ridin' down 'longside o' hit on one o' his fine hosses, an' Ha'ison
ud sit straightah dan evah, an' you couldn' a tol'
wheddah he knowed de footman wuz a sittin'
side o' him er not.

"Dey wuz mighty good to all de people, de
Stantons wuz, an' dey faihly id'lized dem. Why,
ef Miss Dolly had a stahted to put huh foot on
de groun' any time she'd a had a string o' niggers ez long ez f'om hyeah to yandah a layin'

daihse'ves in de paf fu' huh to walk on, fu' dey
sholy did love huh. An' de Cunnel, he wuz de
beatenes' man. He could nevah walk out on de
plantation 'dout a whole string o' piccaninnies a
followin' aftah him. Dey knowed whut dey wuz
doin', fu' aftah while de Cunnel tu'n roun' an'
th'ow 'em a whole lot o' coppers an' fips, an'
bless yore hea't, sich anothah scram'lin' an'
rollin' an' a tumblin' in de dus' you nevah seed.
Well, de Cunnel, he'd stan' thar an' des natchelly
crack his sides a-laffin' ontwell dey wuz thoo
fightin', den he call up dem dat hadn't got nuffin'
an' give 'em daih sheer, so's to see 'em all go off
happy, a-hollerin' 'Thanky, Mas' Stant', thanky,
mastah!' I reckon any fips dey gits now dey
has to scratch fu' wuss'n dey did den. Dem wuz
wunnerful times!

"Den come 'long de time o' de wah, an' den
o' co'se I oughtn' say hit, but de Cunnel, he make
a great big mistake; he freed all de niggahs.
Hit wuz des dis away: de Stantons, dey freed all
daih servants right in de middle o' de wah, an'
o' cose nobody couldn' stan' ag'inst daih wo'd, so
freedom des spread. Mistah Lincoln mought 'a'
been all right, but he didn' have nothin' to do
wid hit. Hit wuz Mas' Stanton, dat who it wuz.

Ef hit wasn', huccome Mas' Stanton keep all de sarvants he want, eben ef he do pay 'em wages? Huccome he keep Ha'ison, 'ceptin' he writ home to his lady? He wuz at de wah, an' thar wasn' no mo folks on de place, 'ceptin' a sarvant, w'en hit all come up. Ha'ison he layin' flat on his back sick in his cabin, an' not able to do nuffin a-tall. Seemed lak dey'd a freed a no-count dahky lak dat; but, no, suh, ol' Mis' sont Marfy to nuss him, an' sont him all kin' o' contraptions to git him well, an' ol' Doctah Ma'maduke Wilson he come to see him.

"Den w'en Ha'ison got up ol' Mis' went down to see him, an' tuk him his wages, an' 'sisted on payin' him fu' de th'ee months he'd been a-layin thar, 'case she said he wuz free an' he'd need all de money he could git. Den Ha'ison, he des broke down, an' cried lak a baby, an' said he nevah 'spected dat ol' Mis' 'ud evah put any sich disgrace erpon him, an' th'owed de money down in de dus' an' fell down on his knees right thar in all his unifo'm.

"Mis' Stanton, she cry, too, an' say she didn' mean no ha'm to him. Den she tell him to git up, an' he 'fuse to git up, 'ceptin she promise dat he allus gwine to drive huh des lak he been doin'.

Den she say she spec' dey gwine to be po', an'
he 'ply to huh dat he don' keer; so she promise,
an' tek de money, an' he git up happy. Dat look
lak de end o' hit all, but la, chile! dat wuz des de
beginnin', an' de end o' hit ain't come yet.

"De middle paht come w'en de wah ended,
an' de ol' Cunnel come back home all broke up
f'om de battles, an' de young mans, dey nevah
come back a-tall. Daih pappy, he wuz mighty
proud o' dem, dough. He'd allus say dat he lef'
his two boys wid daih feet to de foe. I reckon
dat's de way dey bu'y dem. He wuz a invally
hisse'f—dat's what dey call de sojers dat's gone
down in de Valley an' de Shadder o' Def, an' he
sholy wuz in de Valley a long w'ile. But Ha'ison
he des keep on drivin' dem, dough de plantation
wuz all to' up, an' dey'd got mighty po', an' daih
fine ca'iges wuz sold, an' dey didn' have but one
hoss, him a-lookin' lak a ol' crow-bait. Marfy
patched an' patched huh man's lib'ry 'twell hit
wuz one livin' sight to behol'.

"W'en dat ol' crow-bait o' a hoss died, him
an' Marfy wouldn' let daih ol' Mis' go out a-tall,
but Marfy, she'd wheel de Cunnel roun' in his
cheer, w'ile huh man wuz a-hi'in' out so's to buy
anothah hoss an' a spring wagin. Soon's dey got

dat de ol' Missis 'menced comin' back to ch'uch ag'in, 'case she mighty 'ligious ooman, an' allus wuz. An' Ha'ison he sat on dat wagin seat de same ez ef he wuz on de ol' ca'ige.

" 'Ha'ison,' somebody say to him one time, w'yn't you go on away f'om hyeah an' mek somep'n' out yorese'f? You got 'telegence.' Ha'ison, he go 'long an' shet his mouf, an' don' say nuffin'. So dey say ag'in, 'Ha'ison, w'y don' you go 'long up Norf an' git to be a Cong'essman, er somep'n' 'nothah?' Den he say, 'I don' want to be no Cong'essman, ner nuffin else. I been a-drivin' ol' Mis' fu' lo, dese many yeahs, an' I don' want nuffin bettah den des to keep on drivin' huh.' W'y dat man, seemed lak he got proudah dan evah, 'case hit wuzn' de money he wuz lookin' aftah; hit wuz de fambly. Anybody kin git money, but Gawd got to gin yo' quality.

"I don' lak to talk 'bout de res' o' it. But, de spring wagin an' de hoss had to go w'en de Cunnel laid down in de Valley, an' hit wuz nigh onter a yeah fo' ol' Mis' Stanton come out to chu'ch ag'in. But Ha'ison done eahned dat team o' oxen an' de cyart, an' dey been comin' in dat evah sence. She des ez sweet an' ladyfied ez she evah wuz, an' dat niggah des ez proud. I tell you, man, you kin kiver hit up wid rags a foot deep, but dey ain' no way to keep real quality f'om showin' !"

The old man paused and got up, for the forgotten service was over and the people were filing out of church. When the old lady came out there were lifted hats and courtly bows all along her pathway, which she acknowledged with gentle gracefulness. Her coachman suddenly became alive again as he helped her into the rude cart and climbed in beside her. She gave her hand to a slim, fine-faced man as he stopped to bid her good-by, then the oxen turned and moved off up the road whence they had come.

THE EASTER WEDDING.

The brief, sharp winter had passed and Easter was approaching. As Easter Monday was a great day for marrying, Aunt Sukey's patience was entirely worn out with her master's hesitancy, for which she could see no reason. She had long ago given her consent, and young Liza had said "yes" to Ben too many days past to talk about, and the old woman could not see why the white man, the one least concerned, should either object or hesitate. She had lorded it in the family for so long that it now seemed very hard suddenly to be denied anything.

"I tell you, Mas' Lancaster," she said, "dem two chillum been gallantin' wid each othah too long to pa't dem now. How'd you 'a' felt w'en you spa'kin' Mis' Dolly ef somebody 'd 'a' helt you apa't an' kep you fwom ma'yin', huh? Cose I knows you gwine say Ben and 'Lize des niggahs, but la' Mas' you'd be s'prised w'en hit come to lovin', dem two des de same ez white folks in dere feelin's."

It was perhaps this point in the old woman's argument that overcame Robert Lancaster's ob-

jections.   He surrendered and gave his consent
to the marriage of Sukey's Lize and his boy
Ben on the Monday following Easter.   Great
were the rejoicings that attended the announce-
ment of the affair, and because Sukey herself was
a great person on the plantation and Ben his master's valet, the wedding was to be no small one.

As the days passed the preparations were hastened.   The mistress herself went into town and
purchased such a dress as only Sukey's daughter
could have thought of wearing, even though both
Easter and her wedding day came at the same
time.   The young mistress, she who had married
early but was widowed and sad now, had brought
out a once used orange wreath and a veil as filmy
as a fairy spider's web, and both the white
mother and daughter took as deep an interest in
the affair as did the two black women.   While
Sukey and Liza spun and wove they laughed,
chatted and sewed, and they could not understand why Robert Lancaster kept so close to his
library and looked on at all the preparations with
no gladness in his eyes and no mirth on his
tongue.   He was closeted often with strange men
from town, but they thought very little of that.
He was a popular man, and it was not to be won-

dered at that he should be visited by people who did not know him.

It may have been that Robert Lancaster was an arch dissembler or only that he was less transparent than his brother, the good and child-like rector, who cared for the souls of the whole country, and for the bodies of one-half its population and took no thought for the morrow. It was on his face that they first saw the cloud that hung over them all. Robert himself was slow to confess it, and when his wife went to him and taxed him with holding something from her, some trouble on his mind that he was bearing alone, he confessed all, and she took up the burden of it with him. For some time past things had gone badly with him. He had been careless of his crops and over-indulgent with his servants. A man drawn apart from the mere commercial pursuits of life to the quieter world of literature and art, he had paid little attention to the affairs of his plantation, and suddenly he awoke to find his overseer rich and himself poor. Little or nothing was left of all that had been his, except his wife, his daughter and his memories. But what grieved him most was that his slaves, beings whom he had treated almost as his own children, whom he had indulged and spoiled until they were not fit to work for any other master, would have to be put upon the block. He knew what that meant, and felt all the horror of it. He had fostered fidelity among them and he knew that now it would fall back upon them, bringing only suffering and pain, for wives and husbands who had been together for years must be separated and whole families broken up.

"It was for this reason, Dolly," he said, "that I objected to the marriage of Ben and Eliza. They are two, good, whole-souled darkies, and they love each other, I suppose, as well as we ever could have loved, and it seems hard to let them go into the farce of marrying with the chance of being separated again in three or four weeks."

"Won't you be able to keep them anyway, Robert?" asked his wife.

"No, I am sorry I cannot. I shall keep a few of the older servants who would be absolutely useless to a new master, but the greed of my creditors will swallow everything that is of any commercial value."

His wife put her arms about his neck and laid her cheek against his.

"Never mind, Robert," she said, "never mind. We have our Dolly still, and each other. Then there is James, so we shall get on very well, after all."

"But what of Ben and Eliza?"

"Well, let them dream their dream while they may. If the dream be short, it will at least be sweet."

"It is not right," her husband said, "it is not right. It is giving them a false hope which is bound to be dashed when the sale comes."

"Sufficient unto the day is the evil thereof," said his brother James, crossing the threshold. He joined his word to his sister-in-law's, and together they persuaded the broken man to let the marriage go on, to let the two servants sup whatever of joy there might be for them. "Perhaps," added the always sanguine rector, "some man will be good enough to buy the two together. Anyway, we can try."

By an effort his voice was cheerful and his manner buoyant, but on his face there was a deeper shadow than that which clouded the brows of his brother, for now when his all was gone from which so many had received bounty, what would the poor of the county do?"

The sad conversation was hardly finished when Aunt Sukey came in. It was something more that she had to say about "de weddin' fixin's." She was delighted and garrulous.

"Tell you what, Mas' Lancaster," she said, "hit do seem to me lak ol' times agin, all dis fixin' an' ca'in on. 'Pears to me lak de day o' my man Jeems done come back agin. Yo' spe't, yo' mannah an' yo' dispersition an' evahthing des de spittin' image of yo' pa. 'Tain't no wunner day named you Robbut aftah him. I 'membah how he say to me w'en Jeems come a-courtin', 'Sukey,' he say, 'Sukey, you gwine ma'y Jeems right, you gwine ma'y him wid a preachah, an' you gwine to live wid him 'twell you die. Dain't gwine to be no jumpin' ovah de broom an' pa'tin' in a year on my plantation. You gwine to all de famblies. La, bless yo' soul! wen Jeems an' me ma'ied, we had de real preachah dah, an' we stood up an' helt han's an' 'peated ovah, "twell deaf do us pa't,' des lak white folks. It sho did mek me monst'ous happy an' glad w'en I foun' out you gwine to do de same wid 'Lize an' Ben. 'Lize she a good gal, an' Ben be stiddy, an' Mas'

Jeems," she said, turning to the rector, "I know you ain't gwine 'fuse to ma'y 'em out on de po'ch des lak me an' Jeems was ma'ied. Hit'll do my ol' eyes good. I kin o' believe my soul be fit fu' glory den."

The clergyman cleared his throat to speak, but the old woman broke in. "You ain't gwine 'fuse, Mas' Jeems? 'Lize an' Ben dey loves one 'nothah in de real ma'in' way an' dey hea'ts des sot on you jinin' 'em."

The brothers gazed for a moment into each other's eyes, and then James said huskily: "All right, Aunt Sukey, I'll do it."

She went away happy, but over the inmates of the big house a gray pall of sorrow fell.

Easter radiant with flowers and birds and the glorious Southern sunshine came but 'Lize had another use for her holiday dress, and Ben was ashamed to go, so neither of them went to the church service; a gladder, holier service waited for them. There followed a happy Monday, then the night of the wedding came and the long procession of servants marched from Aunt Sukey's cabin in the quarters up to the big house. The porch was garlanded and festooned. Under the farther end, near where the bridal pair would stand, sat the master's family; the dark-robed widow, whose mind went back sadly to her own brief married life, the master, the mistress, and the rector. His face was pale and set, but as the strange, weird wedding song of the Negroes came to his ears and they marched up the steps, stiff, awkward, but proud, in the best clothes they could muster, he tried to call back to his features the far smile which had always been so ready to welcome them. Eliza and Ben led the way. She radiant in her new finery smiling and bridling, Ben shame-faced, head hung and shuffling, and behind them Aunt Sukey in all the glory of a new turban and happy as she had been with her Jeems years and years ago.

They halted before the preacher and he pressed his brother's hand and stood up. The servants gathered around them, eager and expectant. The wedding hymn died away into the night, a low minor sob, as much of sorrow in it as of joy, as if it foreshadowed all that this marriage was and was not. Just as the last faint echo died away into the woods that skirted the lawn and the waiting silence was most intense, the hoot of an owl smote upon their ears and Eliza turned ashen with fear. She gripped Ben's arm; it was the worst of omens. James Lancaster knew the superstitions of the people and as he heard the cry of the evil bird, his book shook in his hand. Was it prophetic? His voice trembled with more than one emotion as he began: "Dearly beloved—"

The ceremony ran on, a deep-toned solo with an accompaniment of the anxious breathing of the onlookers. Then the preacher hesitated. He turned for an instant and looked at his brother, and in the glance was all the agony of a wounded heart. His next words were uttered in a scarcely audible tone, "till death do us part." And after him they all unknowing, repeated, " 'twell deaf do us pa't."

It was over. The couples reformed and followed the bridal pair down the steps, Aunt Sukey hardly containing her joy, but Ben and Eliza somehow subdued. As their feet touched the ground of the lawn, the owl hooted again, and ever and anon, his voice was heard as the procession wound its stately way to the place of the next festivities.

In silence, the family from the big house followed. The two men walked together. As they reached the door of the decorated barn, James paused and took his brother's hand.

"Till death do them part," he cried. "My God! will it be death or the block!" Then with hard, forced smiles, they turned into the room to open the dance and the fiddles struck up a merry tune.

THE FINDING OF MARTHA.

Whether one believes in predestination or not, the intenseness with which Gideon Stone went toward his destiny would have been a veritable and material proof of foreordination. Even before the old mistress had followed her husband to the silent land and the marriage of Miss Ellen had entirely broken up the home, he had begun to exhort among the people who were forming a free community about the old slave plantation. The embargo against negro education having been removed, he learned to read by hook and by crook, and night after night in his lonely room he sat poring over the few books that he could lay his hands upon.

Aside from the semi-pastoral duties which he had laid upon himself, his life was a lonely one. For Gideon was no less true to his love than he had been to his honor. Since Martha had left him, five years before, no other woman had been enshrined in his heart, and the longing was ever in him to go forth and search for her. But his duties and his poverty still held him bound, and so the years glided away. Gideon's powers, however, were not rusting from disuse. He was gaining experience and increasing his knowledge.

It was now that the wave of enthusiasm for the education of the blacks swept most vigorously over the South, and, catching him, carried him into the harbor of one of the new Southern schools. The chief business of these institutions then was the turning out of teachers and preachers. During the months of his vacations Gideon followed the former calling as a means of preparation for the latter. So he was imparting to others the Rule of Three very soon after he had learned it himself. He brought to both these new labors of his the same earnestness and seriousness that had characterized his life on the plantation. And in due course the little school sent him forth proudly as one of her brightest and best.

The course being finished, Gideon's first impulse was to go farther southward, where his duty toward his fellows was plain. But his plan warred with the longing that had been in his heart ever since he had seen the blue lines swing over the hills and away, and he knew that with them Martha was making her way northward. He had never heard of her since; but he did not blame her. She could not write herself, few of her associates could, and in the turmoil of the times it would not be easy to get a letter written, or, being written, get it to him. Not for one moment did he lose faith in her. He believed that somewhere she was waiting for him,—impatiently, perhaps, but still with trust. He would go to her. From that moment his search should begin. Washington was the Mecca for his people then. Perhaps among those who had flocked from the South to the nation's capital he might find the object of his search. It was worth the trying, so thither he turned his steps.

At that time, when the first desire for a minister with at least a little more knowledge than they themselves possessed was coming to the Negroes, it was not a difficult matter for Gideon to find a church. He was called to a small chapel very shortly after he arrived in Washington, and after pastoring that for a few months found himself over the larger congregation of Shiloh Church, which was the mother of his former charge.

He had an enthusiasm for his work that gave him influence over the people and made him popular both as a preacher and a pastor, while

the voice that in the days gone by had sung
"Gideon's Band" was mighty in its aid to the
volunteer choir. His fame grew week by week,
and he drew around him a larger and better
crowd of his own people. But in it all, his oc-
cupations and his successes, he did not forget why
he had come to the city. His eye was ever out
for a glimpse of a familiar face. With no
thought of self-aggrandizement, he yet did all in
his power to spread his name abroad, for,
thought he, "If Martha hears of me, she will
come to me." He did not trust to this method
alone, however, but went forth at all times upon
his search.

"Hit do 'pear to me moughty funny," said one
of his congregation to another one day, "dat a
preachah o' Brothah Stone's ability do hang erroun' de deepo so."

"Hang erroun' de deepo! What you talkin'
'bout, Sis Mandy?"

"Dat des whut I say. Dat man kin sholy
allus be foun' at one deepo er anothah, Sis Lizy."

"I don't know how dat come, case he sholy do
mek his pasto'ial wisits."

"I ain't 'sputin' de wisits, ner I ain't a-blamin'
de man, case I got all kin' o' faif in Brothah

Gidjon Stone, but I do say, an' dey's othahs dat kin tell you de same, dat w'en he ain't a-wisitin' de sick er a-preachin', he stan' erroun' watchin' de steam-cyahs, an' dey say his eyes des glisten w'enevah a train comes in."

"Huh, uh, honey, dey's somep'n' behime dat."

" 'Tain't fu' me to say. Cose I knows all edjicated people has dey cuhiousnesses, but dis is moughty cuhious."

It was indeed true, as Sister Mandy Belknap had said, that Gideon was often to be found at one or the other of the railway stations, where he watched feverishly the incoming and outgoing trains. Maybe Martha would be on one of them. She might be coming in or going out any day, and so he was miserable whenever he missed a day at his post. The station officials looked in wonder at the slim Negro in clerical dress who came day by day to watch with intense face the monotonous bustle of arrival and departure. Whoever he is, they thought, he has been expecting someone for a long time.

The trains went and the trains came, and yet Martha did not appear, and the eager look in Gideon's face grew stronger. The intent gaze with which he regarded the world without grew keener and more expectant. It was as if all the yearning that his soul had experienced in all the years had come out into his face and begged pity of the world. And yet there was none of this plea for pity in Gideon's attitude. On the contrary, he went his own way, and a brave, manly way it was, that asked less of the world than it gave. The very disappointment which he restrained made him more helpful to the generally disappointed and despised people to whom he ministered. When his heart ached within him, he took no time for repining, but measuring their pain by his own, set out to find some remedy for their suffering. Their griefs were mirrored in his own sorrow, and every wail of theirs was but the echo of his own heart's cry. He drew people to him by the force of his sympathetic understanding of their woes, and even those who came for his help and counsel went away asking how so young a man could feel and know so much.

Meanwhile in Gideon's congregation a feeling of unrest seemed taking possession of the sisters. In the privacy of their families they spoke of the matter which troubled them to indifferent husbands, who guffawed and went their several ways as if a momentous question were not taxing their wives' minds. But the women would not be put off. When they found that the men, with the indifference of the sex, refused to be interested, they talked among themselves, and they concluded without a dissenting voice that there was something peculiar, something strange and uncanny, about the celibacy of the Reverend Gideon Stone. He was abnormal. He was the shining exception in a much-marrying calling.

A number of them were gathered at Sister Mandy Belknap's home one Friday evening, when the conversation turned to the preacher's unaccountable course.

"Hit seem mo' unnatchul lak, case preachahs is mos'ly de marryinest kin' o' men," said Sister Lizy Doke.

"To be sho'; dat what mek his diffuntness look so cuhious."

"Well, now, look-a-hyeah, sistahs," spoke up a widow lady who was now enjoying a brief interval of single-blessedness after a stormy parting with her fourth spouse; "don't you reckon dat man got a wife som'ers? You know men will do dat thing. I 'membah my third husban'.

W'en I ma'ied him he had a wife in Tennessee, and anothah one in Fuginny. I know men."

"Brothah Gidjon ain't nevah been ma'ied," said Sister Mandy shortly.

"Huccome you so sho'?"

"He ain't got de look; dat's huccome me so sho'?"

"Huh, uh, honey, dey ain't no tellin' whut kin' o' look a man kin put on. I know men, I tell you."

"Brothah Gidjon ain't ma'ied," reiterated the hostess; "fust an' fo'mos', dey ain't no foolin' de pusson on de ma'ied look, an' he ain't got it. Den he ain't puttin' on no looks, case Brothah Gidjon is diffunt f'om othah men mo' ways den one. I knows dat ef I is only got my fust husban' an' is still livin' wid him."

The widow lady instantly subsided.

"You don' reckon Brothah Gidjon's been tekin' up any dese hyeah Cath'lic notions, does you?" ventured another speaker. "You know dem Cath'lic pries'es don' nevah ma'y."

"How's he gwine to have any Cath'lic notions, w'en he bred an' born an' raised in de Baptis' faif?"

"Dey ain't no tellin'. Dey ain't no tellin'. W'en colo'ed folks git to gwine to colleges, you nevah know what dey gwine lu'n. My mammy's sistah was sol' inter Ma'ylan', an', bless yo' soul, she's a Cath'lic to dis day."

"Well, I don' know nuffin' 'bout dat, but hit ain't no Cath'lic notions, I tell you. Brothah Gidjon Stone's too solid fu' dat. Dey's some'p'n else behime it."

The interest and curiosity of the women, now that they were fired, did not stop at these private discussions among themselves. They went even farther and broached the matter to the minister.

They suggested jocosely, but with a deep vein of earnestness underlying the statement, that they were looking for a wife for him. But they could elicit from him no response save "There's time enough; oh, there's time enough."

Gideon said this with an appearance of cheerfulness, but in his heart he did not believe it. He did not think that there was time. His body, his mind, his soul all yearned hotly for the companionship of the woman he loved. There are some men born to be husbands, just as there are some men born to be poets, painters, or musicians —men who, living alone, cannot know life.

The Finding of Martha

Gideon was one of these. Every instinct of his being drove him towards domestic life with unflagging insistency. But it was Martha whom he wanted. Martha whom he loved and with whom he had plighted his troth. What to him were the glances of other women? What the seduction in their eyes, and the unveiled invitation in their smiles? There was one woman in the world to him, and she loomed so large to his sight that he could see no other. How he waited; how he longed; how he prayed! And the days passed, the trains came and went, and still no word, no sight of Martha.

Strangers came to his church, and visitors from other cities came to him, and still nothing of her for whom he waited to make his life complete. Then one day in the silence of his own sorrow he fell upon his knees, crying, "My God, my God, why hast thou forsaken me?" And from then hope fled from him. She was dead. She must be, or she would have come to him. He had waited long, oh, so long, and now it was all over. For the rest of his days he must walk the way of his life alone or—could he, could he turn his eyes upon another woman? No, no, his heart cried out to him, and he felt in that moment as a man standing beside his wife's bier would feel should the thought of another obtrude itself.

He went to the trains no more. He searched no more; hope was dead; but the one object that had blinded him, that had given him single sight, being removed, he began to look around him and to see—at first it seemed almost a revelation—other women. Now he saw too their glances and their smiles. He heard the tender notes in their voices as they spoke to him, for all other sounds were no longer drowned by Martha's calling to him from the Unknown. When first he found himself giving fuller range to his narrow vision, he was startled, then apologetic, then defiant. The man in him triumphed. Martha was dead. He was alone. Must he always be? Was life, after all, to be but this bitter husk to him when he had but to reach forth his hand to find the kernel of it?

He had never even been troubled with such speculations before, but now he awoke to the fact that he was not yet old and that the long stretch of life before him looked dreary enough if he must tread it by himself.

In this crisis the tempter, who is always an opportunist, came to Gideon. Sister Mandy Belknap had always manifested a great deal of interest in the preacher's welfare, a surprising amount for a woman who had no daughter. However, she had a niece. Now she came to the pastor with a grave face.

"Brothah Stone," she said, "I got some talk fu' you."

"Yes, Sister Belknap?" said Gideon, settling himself complacently, with the expectation of hearing some tale of domestic woe or some history of spiritual doubt, for among his congregation he was often the arbiter in such affairs.

"Now, I's ol' enough fu' yo' mothah," Sister Mandy went on, and at the words the minister became suddenly alert, for from her introduction her visit seemed to be admonitory, rather than appealing. Evidently he was not to give advice, but to be advised. He was not to be the advocate, but the defendant; not the judge, but the culprit.

"I's seed mo' of life den you has, Brothah Gidjon, ef I do say hit myse'f."

"Not a doubt of it, my sister."

"An' I knows mo' 'bout men an' women den you does. Co'se you know mo' 'bout Scripter den I does, dough I ricollect dat de Lawd said dat it ain't good fu' man to be alone."

Gideon started. It was as if the old woman had by some occult power divined the trend of his thoughts and come to take part in the direction of them.

"The Bible surely says that, Sister Belknap," he said when the first surprise was over.

"It do, an' I want to know ef you ain't a-flyin' in de face o' Providence by doin' what hit say ain't good fu' a man?"

Gideon was a little bit puzzled, but in answer he began, "There are circumstances——"

"Dat's des' hit," said Sister Mandy impressively; "sarcumstances, sarcumstances, an' evah man dat wants to disobey de wo'd t'inks he's got de sarcumstances. Uh! I tell you de ol' boy is a moughty clevah han' at mekin' excuses fu' us."

"I don't reckon, sister, that we've got the same point of view," said Gideon nervously.

" 'Tain't my p'int of view, 'tain't mine; hit's de Lawd A'mighty's. You young, Brothah Gidjon, you young, an' you don' see lak I does, but lemme tell you, hit ain't right fu' no man whut ain't ma'ied to be a-pasto'n no sich a flock. I don' want to meddle into yo' business, but all I got to say is, you bettah look erroun' you an' choose a wife fu' to be yo' he'pmeet. 'Scuse me fu' speakin' to you, Brothah. Go 'roun' an' see my niece. She kin p'int out some moughty nice women."

"It was mighty good of you to speak, and I am glad that you came to me. I will think over what you have said."

" 'It is not good for man to be ·alone,' " mused Gideon when his visitor was gone. Was not this just the word of help and encouragement that he had wanted—indeed, the one that he had been waiting for? He had been faithful, he told himself. He had looked and he had waited. Martha had not come, and was it not true that "it is not good for man to be alone?" He went to bed that night with the sentence ringing in his head.

Mandy Belknap had done her work well, for on the following Sunday the preacher smiled on her niece, Caroline Martin, and on the Sunday after that he walked home to dinner with her.

What the gossips said about it at the time, how they gazed and chattered, and with what a feeling of self-satisfaction Sister Mandy went her way, are details that do not belong to this story. However, one cannot pass over Gideon's attitude in this new matter. It is true that he found himself liking Caroline better and better the more frequently he saw her. The girl's pretty ways pleased him. She was a member of his choir, and he thought often how like Martha's her voice was. Indeed, he was wont to compare her with this early love of his, and it did not occur to him that he cared for her not so much for what she was herself, but for the few points in which she resembled his lost sweetheart. He was not wooing (if wooing his attentions could be called) Caroline Martin as Caroline Martin, but only as a proxy for his own unforgotten Martha, for even now, in the face of hopelessness, his love and faith were stronger than he.

Caroline Martin was the most envied girl in Shiloh Church, for, indeed, hers was no slight distinction, to be singled out by the minister for his special attention after so long a period of indifference. But envy and gossip passed her by as the idle wind, for the very honor which had been accorded her placed her above the reach of petty jealousies. Her triumph, however, was to be brief.

It was on a rainy Sunday night in October, a late Washington October, which has in it all the possibilities of nastiness given to weather. Shiloh Chapel was well filled despite the storm without. Gideon was holding forth in his accustomed way, vigorously, eloquently, and convincingly. His congregation was warming up to a keen appreciation of his sermon, when suddenly the door opened, and a drabbled, forlornlooking woman entered and sank into a back seat. One glance at her, and the words died on Gideon's lips. He paused for a moment and swayed upon his feet while his heart beat a wild tattoo.

It was Martha, his Martha, but, oh, how sadly changed! His heart fell a-bleeding for her as he saw the once proud woman sitting there crouched in her seat among the well-dressed people like the humblest of creatures. He wanted to stop right there in the midst of his sermon and go rushing to her, to take her in his arms and tell her that if the world had dealt hard with her, he at least was true.

It was a long pause he made, and the congregation was looking at him in surprise. Then he recovered himself, and went on with his exhortation, hastily, feverishly. He could scarcely wait to be done.

The last words of the benediction fell from his lips and he hastened down the aisle, elbowing his way through the detaining crowd, his face set toward one point. Someone spoke to him as he passed, but he did not hear; a hand was stretched out to him, but he did not see it. There was but one thought in his mind.

He reached the seat in the corner of which Martha had crouched. She was gone. He stood for a moment dazed, and then dashed out into the rain and darkness. Nothing was to be seen of her, and hatless he ran on down the street, hoping to strike the direction in which she had started and so overtake her. But she had evidently gone directly across the street or turned another way. Sad and dejected and wondering somewhat, he retraced his steps to the church.

It was Martha; there could be no doubt of that. But why such an act from her? It seemed as if she had purposely avoided him. What had he done to her that she should treat him thus? She must have some reason. It was not like Martha. Yes, there was some good reason, he knew. Faith came back to him then. He had seen her. She was living and he would see her again. His heart lightened and bounded. Martha was found.

Sister Belknap was waiting for him when he got back to the church door, and beside her the comely Caroline.

"Wy, Brothah Gidjon," said the elder woman, "what's de mattah wid you to-night? You des shot outen de do' lak a streak o' lightnin', an' baih-headed, ez I live! I lay you'll tek yo' death o' col' dis hyeah night."

"I saw an old friend of mine from the South in church and I wanted to catch her before she got away, but she was gone."

There was something in the minister's voice, a tone or an inflection, that disturbed Sister Belknap's complacency, and with a sharp, "Come on, Ca'line," she bade him good-night and went her way. He saw them go off together without a pang. As he got his hat and started home, his only thought was of Martha and how she would come again, and he was happy.

The next Sunday he watched every new-comer to the church with eager attention, and so at night; but Martha was not among them. Sunday after Sunday told the same story, and again Gideon's heart failed him. Maybe Martha did not want to see him. Maybe she was married, and his heart grew cold at that.

For over a month, however, his vigilance did not relax, and finally his faith was rewarded. In the midst of his sermon he saw Martha glide in and slip into a seat. He ended quickly, and leaving the benediction to be pronounced by a "local preacher," he hurried down the aisle and was at her side just as she reached the door ahead of everyone.

"Martha, Martha, thank the Lord!" he cried, taking her hand.

"Oh Gid—I mean Brothah—er—Reverent —I must go 'long." The woman was painfully embarrassed.

"I am going with you," he said firmly, still holding her hand as he led her protesting from the church.

"Oh, you mustn't go with me," she cried, shrinking from him.

"Why, Martha, what have I done to you? I've been waiting for you so long."

She had begun to sob now, and Gideon, without pausing to think whether she were married or not, put his arm tenderly about her. "Tell me what it is, Martha? What has kept you from me so long?"

"I ain't no fittin' pusson fu' you now, Gidjon."

"What is it? You're not—are you married?"

"No."

"Have you kept the light?"

"Yes, thank de Lawd, even wid all my low-downness, I's kept de light in my soul."

"Then that's all, Martha?"

"No, it ain't—it ain't. I wouldn't stay wid you w'en you axed me, an' I came up hyeah an' got po'er an' po'er, an' dey's been times w'en I ain't had nothin' ha'dly to go on; but I wouldn't sen' you no wo'd, case I was proud an' I was ashamed case I run off to fin' so much an' only foun' dis. Den I hyeahed dat you was edjicated an' comin' hyeah to preach. Dat made you furder away f'om me, an' I knowed you wasn' fu' me no mo'. It lak to killed me, but I stuck it out. Many an' many's de time I seen you an' could 'a' called you, but I thought you'd be ashamed o' me."

"Martha!"

"I wouldn' 'a' come to yo' chu'ch, but I wanted to hyeah yo' voice ag'in des once. Den I wouldn' 'a' come back no mo', case I thought you reckernized me. But I had to—I had to. I was hongry to hyeah you speak. But go back now, Gidjon, I'm near home, an' I can't tek you to dat po' place."

But Gideon marched right on. A light was in his face and a springiness in his step that had been absent for many a day. She halted before a poor little house, two rooms at the most, the front one topped with a stove-pipe which did duty as a chimney.

"Hyeah's whaih I live," she said shamefacedly; "you would come."

They went in. The little room, ill furnished, was clean and neat, and the threadbare carpet was scrupulously swept.

Gideon had been too happy to speak, but now he broke silence. "This is just about the size of the cabin we'd have had if the war hadn't come on. Can you get ready by to-morrow?"

The Finding of Martha

"No, no, I ain't fu' you, Gidjon. I ain't got nothin'. I don't know nothin' but ha'd work. What would I look lak among yo' fine folks?"

"You'd look like my Martha, and that's what you're going to do."

Her eyes began to shine. "Gidjon, you don't mean it! I thought when colo'ed folks got edjicated dey fu'got dey mammys an' dey pappys an' dey ol' frien's what can't talk straight."

"Martha," said Gideon, "did you ever hear 'Nearer, my God, to Thee' played on a banjo?"

"No."

"Well, you know the instrument isn't much, but it's the same sweet old tune. That's the way it is when old friends tell me their love and friendship brokenly. Can't you see?"

They talked long that night, and Gideon brought Martha to his way of thinking, though she held out for less haste. She exacted a week.

On the following Sunday the Reverend Gideon Stone preached as his congregation had never heard him preach before, and after the service, being asked to remain, they were treated to a surprise that did their hearts good. A brother pastor, mysteriously present, told their story and performed the ceremony between Gideon and Martha.

So many of them were just out of slavery. So many of them knew what separation and fruitless hope of re-meeting were, that it was an event to strike home to their hearts. Some wept, some rejoiced, and all gathered around the pastor and his wife to grasp their hands.

And then Martha was back on the old plantation again and her love and Gideon's was young, and she never knew why she did it, but suddenly her voice, the voice that Gideon had loved, broke into one of the old plantation hymns. He joined her. Members from the old South threw back their heads, and, seeing the yellow fields, the white cabins, the great house, in the light of other days, fell into the chorus that shook the church, and people passing paused to listen, saying,—

"There's a great time at Shiloh to-day."

And there was.

THE DEFECTION OF MARIA ANN GIBBS.

There had been a wonderful season of grace at Bethel Chapel since the advent of the new minister, and the number of converts who had entered the fold put the record of other years and other pastors to shame. Seats that had been empty were filled; collections that had been meagre were now ample. The church had been improved; a coat of paint had been put on the outside, and the interior had been adorned by a strip of carpet down the two aisles and pink calcimining on the walls. The Rev. Eleazar Jackson had proved a most successful shepherd. The fact was shown by the rotundity of his form, which bespoke good meals, and the newness of his clothes, which argued generous contributions.

He was not only a very eloquent man, but had social attainments of a high order. He was immensely popular with the sisters, and was on such good terms with the brothers that they forgot to be jealous of him. When he happened around about an hour before dinner-time, and

some solicitous sister killed for him the fattening
fowl which her husband had been watching with
eager eyes, Mr. Jackson averted any storm which
might have followed by such a genial presence
and such a raciness of narration at the table that
the head of the house forgot his anger and
pressed the preacher to have some more of the
chicken.

Notwithstanding this equality of regard on
the part of both brothers and sisters, it was yet
noticeable that the larger number of the converts
were drawn from the tenderer sex—but human
nature is human nature, women are very much
women, and the preacher was a bachelor.

Among these gentle converts none was more
zealous, more ardent or more constant than
Maria Ann Gibbs. She and her bosom friend,
Lucindy Woodyard, had "come th'oo" on the
same night, and it was a wonderful event. They
shouted all over Bethel Chapel. When one went
up one aisle the other came down the other.
When one cried "Hallelujah!" the other shouted
"Glory!" When one skipped the other jumped,
and finally they met in front of the altar, and
binding each other in a joyous embrace, they
swayed back and forth to the rhythm of the

hymn that was rising even above their own rejoicings, and which asserted that,

> "Jedgement Day is a-rollin' round',
> Er how I long to be there!"

It was a wonderfully affecting sight, and it was not long before the whole church was in a tumult of rejoicings. These two damsels were very popular among their people, and every young man who had looked with longing eyes at Lucindy, or sighed for the brown hand of Maria Ann, joined in the shouting, if he was one of the "saved," or, if he was not, hastened up to fall prostrate at the mourners' bench. Thus were the Rev. Eleazar Jackson's meetings a great success, and his name became great in the land.

From the moment of their conversion Lucindy and Maria Ann went hand in hand into the good work for the benefit of the church, and they were spoken of as especially active young members. There was not a sociable to be given, nor a donation party to be planned, nor a special rally to be effected, but that these two consulted each other and carried the affair to a successful issue. The Rev. Eleazar often called attention

to them in his exhortations from the pulpit, spoke
of the beautiful harmony between them, and
pointed it out as an example to the rest of his
flock. He had a happy turn for phrase-making,
which he exercised when he called the two "twin
sisters in the great new birth o' grace."

For a year the church grew and waxed strong,
and the minister's power continued, and peace
reigned. Then as the rain clouds creep slowly
over the mountain-top and bring the storm thun-
dering down into the valley, so ominous signs
began to appear upon the horizon of Bethel's
religious and social life. At first these warning
clouds were scarcely perceptible; in fact, there
were those unbelievers who said that there would
be no storm; but the mutterings grew louder.

The first sign of danger was apparent in the
growing coolness between Lucindy and Maria
Ann. They were not openly or aggressively
enemies, but from being on that high spiritual
plane, where the outward signs of fellowship
were not needed, and on which they called each
other by their first names, they had come down
to a level which required, to indicate their relations one to the other, the interchange of "Sister Gibbs" and "Sister Woodyard." There had

been a time when they had treated each other with loving and familiar discourtesy, but now they were scrupulously polite. If one broke in upon the other's remarks in church council, it was with an "Excuse me, Sis' Gibbs," or "I beg yo' pa'don, Sis' Woodyard," and each seemed feverishly anxious to sacrifice herself to make way for the other.

Then they came to work no more together. The separation was effected without the least show of anger. They simply drifted apart, and Lucindy found herself at the head of one faction and Maria Ann in the lead of another. Here for a time a good-natured rivalry was kept up, much to the increase of Bethel's finances and its minister's satisfaction. But an uncertain and less genial note began to creep into these contests as the Rev. Eleazar Jackson continued to smile upon both the ardent sisters.

The pastor at Bethel had made such a glowing record as a financier that the Bishop had expressed his satisfaction by a special letter, and requested that at the June rally he make an extra effort to raise funds for the missionary cause. Elated at this mark of distinction, and with visions of a possible Presiding Eldership in his mind, Mr. Jackson sought out his two most attractive parishioners and laid his case before them. It was in the chapel, immediately after the morning service, that he got them together.

"You see, sisters," he said, "Bethel have made a record which she have to sustain. She have de reputation o' bein' one o' the most lib'l chu'ches in de Confer'nce. Now we don't want to disa'point the Bishop when he picks us out to help him in such a good cause. O' co'se I knowed who I could depend on, an' so I come right to you sisters to see if you couldn't plan out some'p'n that would make a real big splurge at de June rally."

He paused and waited for the sisters to reply. They were both silent. This made him uneasy, and he said, "What you think, Sister Gibbs?"

"Oh," said Maria Ann, "I'm waitin' to hyeah f'om Sis' Woodyard."

"Oh, no," said Sister Woodyard politely, "don' wait on me, Sis' Gibbs. 'Spress yo'se'f, 'spress yo'se'f."

But Maria Ann still demurred. "I couldn't think o' puttin' my po' opinions up 'fo' Sis Woodyard," she said. "I'd a good deal ruther wait

The Defection of Maria Ann Gibbs

to hyeah f'om my elders." She laid especial
stress on the last word.

Lucindy smiled a smile so gentle that it was
ominous.

"I ain't holdin' back 'ecause I cain't think o'
nothin'," she said, "but jes' 'ecause I ain't been
used to puttin' myse'f forrard, an' I don't like to
begin it so late." And she smiled again.

The minister began to feel uneasy. Figura-
tively speaking, both of the sisters seemed to be
sparring for wind, and he thought it better to
call the council to a close and see each one
separately.

"Well," he said hurriedly, "I know you sisters
will come to some conclusion, an' jes' 'po't to me
on next Wednesday night, an' I will pass a kind
o' 'view over yo' plans, an' offer a su'jestion,
mebbe. We want to do some'p'n that will bring
out de people an' mek 'em give gen'ously of their
means for de benefit o' de heathen."

The two sisters bowed very politely to each
other, shook the minister's hand, and went their
different ways.

It must have been Satan himself who effected
the result of having both women hit upon the
same plan of action. Maria Ann was pleased

at her idea, and hastened to church on Wednesday evening to report it to the pastor, only to find that Lucindy Woodyard had been before her with the same plan.

"I mus' congratulate you, sisters," said the Rev. Eleazar, "bofe upon yo' diligence an' yo' fo'thought. It must 'a' been P'ovidence that directed bofe yo' min's in de same channel."

Both the sisters were aghast. They had both suggested dividing the church into soliciting parties and giving a prize to the one collecting the highest amount of money. Perhaps the Devil was not so much concerned in making their minds revert to this as it appeared, as it is a very common device for raising money among negro churches. However, both the women were disappointed.

"I'd jes' leave draw out an' let Sis' Gibbs go on an' manage dis affair," said Lucindy.

"I'd ruther be excused," said Maria Ann, "an' leave it in Sis' Woodyard's han's."

But the minister was wily enough to pour oil on the troubled waters, and at the same time to suggest a solution of the problem that would enlist the sympathies and ambition of both the women.

The Defection of Maria Ann Gibbs

"Now I su'jest," he said, "that bofe you sisters remains in dis contest, an' then, instid o' throwin' the competition open, you sisters by yo'se'ves each be de head o' a pa'ty that shall bring de money to you, an' the one of you that gets the most f'om her pa'ty shall have de prize."

Lucindy's eyes glittered, and Maria Ann's flashed, as they agreed to the contest with joyful hearts. Here should be a trial of both strength and prowess, and it would be shown who was worthy to walk the ways of life side by side with the Rev. Eleazar Jackson.

Joyfully they went to their tasks. Their enthusiasm inspired their followers with partisan energy. Side bantered side, and party taunted party, but the leaders kept up a magnificent calm. It was not they alone who knew that there was more at stake than the prize that was offered, that they had more in view than the good of the heathen souls. There were other eyes that saw and minds that understood besides those of Lucindy, Maria Ann and the preacher.

Pokey Williams, who was very warm in the Gibbs faction, called from the fence to her neighbor, Hannah Lewis, who was equally ardent on the other side: "How yo' collection come on, Sis' Lewis?"

"Oh, middlin', middlin'; de w'ite folks I wok fu' done p'omise me some'p'n, my grocery man he gwine give me some'p'n, an' I got fo' dollahs in little bits a'ready."

"Oomph," said Pokey, "you jes' boun' an' 'termine to ma'y Lucindy Woodyard to de preachah!"

"G'way f'om hyeah, Pokey, you is de beatenes'! How you gittin' on?"

"Heish, gal, my w'ite folks done gi' me ten dollahs a'ready, an' I'm jes' tacklin' evahbody I know."

"Ten dollahs! W'y, dey ain' no way fu' de preachah to git erway f'om Maria Ann Gibbs ef you keep on!"

The two waved their hands at each other and broke into a rollicking laugh.

The rally in June was the greatest the annals of Bethel Chapel had ever recorded. The prize decided upon was a gold watch, and on the evening that the report and decision were to be made, a hall had to be procured, for the chapel would not hold the crowd. A brief concert was given first to get the people in a good humor,

and to whet their anxiety, and though the per-
formers were well received, little attention was
paid to them, for every one was on the *qui vive*
for the greater drama of the evening. The minister was in his glory.

When the concert was over, he welcomed
Lucindy and Maria Ann to the stage, where they
sat, one on either side of him. The reports
began. First one from Lucindy's side, then one
from Maria Ann's, and so alternately through.
It was very close! The people were leaning forward, eager and anxious for the issue. The reports came thick and fast, and the excitement
grew as the sums increased. The climax was to
be the reports of the two leaders themselves, and
here Lucindy had shown her shrewdness. Maria
Ann's side had begun to report first, and so their
leader was compelled to state her amount first.
There was a certain little reserve fund in the
pocket of her opponent with which young Mrs.
Worthington was somewhat acquainted, and it
was to be used in case Maria Ann should excel
her. Maria Ann made her report, reading from
her book:

" 'Codin' to de returns made by my pa'ty,
which you hev all hyeahed, they hev collected

one hun'erd an' eight dollahs; addin' to that
what I hev collected by myse'f, fifty-two dollahs,
I returns to de chu'ch one hun'erd an' sixty dollahs."

Down in her lap Lucindy did some quick, surreptitious writing. Then she stood up.

" 'Co'din' to de returns which my pa'ty hev
made, an' which you hev all hyeahed, they hev
collected one hun'erd an' two dollahs, an' I, by
my own individual effort"—she laid wonderful
emphasis upon the last two words, "bring in sixty
dollahs, mekin' the total one hun'erd and sixty-
two dollahs, which I submit to de chu'ch."

There was a burst of applause from Lucindy's
partisans, but Maria Ann was on her feet:

"I forgot," she said, "de last donation I received. Mrs. Jedge Haines was kin' enough to
give me a check fu' ten dollahs, which I didn't
add in at fust, an' it brings my collection up to
one hun'erd an' seventy dollahs."

The volume of applause increased at Maria
Ann's statement, but it wavered into silence as
Lucindy arose. She smiled down upon Maria
Ann.

"I'm mighty thankful to de sister," she said,
"fu' mindin' me o' some'p'n I mos' nigh fu'got.

The Defection of Maria Ann Gibbs

Mis' Cal'ine Worthington desired to put her name down on my book fu' twenty dollahs, which brings my collection to one hun'erd an' eighty dollahs."

Mrs. Worthington looked across at Mrs. Haines and smiled. That lady raised her chin. An ashen hue came into Maria Ann Gibbs' face.

With great acclamation the watch was awarded to Lucindy Woodyard, and in congratulating her the Rev. Eleazar Jackson held her hand perhaps a little longer than usual. Mrs. Worthington was standing near at the time.

"If I had known it meant this," she said to herself, "I wouldn't have given her that twenty dollars." The lady saw that she was likely to lose a good servant. When the meeting was out the preacher walked home with Lucindy.

On the following Thursday night the Afro-American Sons and Daughters of Hagar gave a dance at their hall on Main Street. Maria Ann Gibbs, the shining light of Bethel Church, went, and she danced. Bethel heard and mourned.

On the next Sunday she went to church. She walked in with Mose Jackson, who was known to be a sinner, and she sat with him near the door, in the seat of the sinners.

In Old Plantation Days

The Rev. Eleazar Jackson went past Lucindy's house and they walked to church together. Lucindy had increased her stock of jewelry, not only by the watch, but by a bright gold ring which she wore on the third finger of her left hand. But if Maria Ann cared, she did not show it. She had found in the tents of the wicked what she could not get in the temple of the Lord.

A JUDGMENT OF PARIS.

It is a very difficult thing at any time and in any place to be the acknowledged arbiter of social affairs. But to hold this position in "Little Africa" demanded the maximum of independence, discretion and bravery. I say bravery, because the civilization of "Little Africa" had not arrived at that edifying point where it took disapproval gracefully and veiled its feelings. It was crude and primitive, and apt to resent adverse comment by an appeal to force, not of the persuasive but of the vindictive kind.

It had fallen to the lot of Mr. Samuel Hatfield to occupy this delicate position of social judge, and though certain advantages and privileges accrued to him his place was in no wise a sinecure. There were times when his opinions on matters of great moment had been openly scoffed at, and once it had even happened when a decision of his had been displeasing that fleetness of foot alone had saved him from the violence of partisans. Little did it matter to the denizens of "Little Africa" that others might be put upon committees to serve with Mr. Hatfield in judging the merits of waltzers or of the qualities of rival quartets. He was the one who invariably brought in the report and awarded the prize, and on him fell the burden of approval or disapproval.

For some months he had gone on gloriously unannoyed, with no one to judge, and nothing to pass upon. In the absence of these duties, Cupid had stepped in and with one shaft laid him prone at the feet of Miss Matilda Jenkins. Of course, Mr. Hatfield did cast occasional glances at the charms of Miss Amarilla Jones, but Cupid, grown wise with the wisdom of the world, has somehow learned to tip his arrows with gold, and the wound of these is always fatal.

Now, the charms of these two maidens were equal, their brown beauty about the same, but Matilda Jenkins' father was a magnate in "Little Africa," and so———.

On a night in autumn the devil appeared to certain members of the trustees' board of Mt. Moriah Church, and said unto them: "You need money wherewith to run this church," and they answered and said: "Yes, good devil, we do."

The devil spoke again and said: "Give a calico

festival and a prize to the woman wearing the prettiest calico dress." And much elated, they replied: "Yea, verily."

Thereupon the devil, his work being done, vanished with a crafty smile, leaving them to their deliberations.

Brother Jenkins and Brother Jones were both members of the "Boa'd," and when the contest was decided upon they looked across at each other with defiance shining in their eyes, because there was a strong rivalry between the two families. But there animosity apparently ended. Brother Jenkins dropped his eyes, for he was a little old man, and Brother Jones was "husky," which is the word that in their community indicated rude strength. The fight, however, for fight it was going to be, was on.

Within the next few days the shopkeepers of the town sold bolt upon bolt of calico. The buying of this particular line of goods was so persistent that one shopkeeper, who was a strong-tongued, rude man, laid it at the door of certain advocates of industrial education and began to denounce any doctrines which repressed in the negro his love of clothes far above his pocket, and thereby lowered profits.

As soon as Mr. Hatfield learned what was going on he became alarmed, for he saw more clearly than most people and he knew that it was all the invention of the devil. His good angel prompted him to flee from the town at once, but he lingered to think about it, and while he lingered the committee came upon him. They wanted him to be chairman of the awarding committee. He stammered and made excuses.

"You see, gent'mens, hit's des disaway. I 'low I got to go out o' town fu' my boss des 'bout de time dat dis hyeah's comin' off, an' I wouldn' lak to p'omise an' den disap'pint you."

"Dat's all right, dat's all right," said brother Jones, the spokesman; "I knows yo' boss, an' he teks a mighty intrus' in Mt. Moriah. I'll see him an' see ef he can't let you go befo' er after de en'tainment."

The sweat broke out on Mr. Hatfield's brow in painful beads.

"Oh, nevah min', nevah min'," he exclaimed hastily; "dis hyeah's private business, an' I wouldn' lak him to know dat I done spoke 'bout it."

"But we got to have you, Mr. Hatfield. You

sholy mus' speak to yo' boss. Ef you don't, I'll have to."

"I speak to him, den, I speak to him. I see what he say."

"Den I reckon we kin count on yo' suhvices?"

"I reckon you kin," said the victim.

As the committee went its way, Hatfield was sure that he heard a diabolical chuckle and smelt sulphur.

The days that had dragged flew by and the poor social arbiter looked upon the nearing festivity as upon the approach of doom. With the clear perception of a man who knows his world, Mr. Hatfield already saw that all women in the contest besides Matilda Jenkins and Amarilla Jones were but figureheads, accessories only to the real fight between the rival belles. So, as an earnest of his intention to be impartial, he ceased for the time his attentions to Matilda Jenkins. This lady, though, was also wise in her day and generation. She offered no protest at the apparent defection of her lover. Indeed, when her father squeaked his disapproval of Hatfield's action, she was quick to come to his defense.

"I reckon Mr. Hatfield knows what he's about," she said loyally. "You know how de people talks erroun' hyeah. Den, ef he go an' gi' me de prize, dey des boun' to say dat it ain't 'cause I winned it, but 'cause he keepin' comp'ny wid me, an' ain't gwine to shame his own lady."

"Uh, huh," said the old man; "dat hadn't crost my min' befo'."

In the meantime a similar council was taking place between Miss Amarilla Jones and her father.

"I been noticin'," said the paternal Jones one day, "dat Sam Hatfield don' seem to be a-gwine wid Matildy Jenkins so much."

Amarilla modestly ducked—yes, that's the word—she ducked her head, but she smiled as she replied: "Mistah Hatfiel' been cas'in' sheep's-eyes at me fu' a long while now."

"Well, what good do dat do, less'n he up an' say some'p'n?"

"Nevah you min', pap; I 'lows I un'erstan' young men bettah dan you do. Ef he don' mean nuffin, how come he done give up Matildy Jenkins des at dis junction?"

"Hit's all mighty quare to me."

"Don' you see he got to jedge de contes', an' he cain't go ag'in his own lady, so he gin huh up?

Now, ef he gi' me de prize, he feel puffectly free to ax me to ma'y him."

"Whew-ee!" whistled the elder, entirely overcome with admiration at his daughter's sagacity; "you sholy has got a quick head on dem shoulders o' yo'n!"

At the time appointed the members and friends of Mt. Moriah assembled for the calico social. The church was crowded with a curiously-gowned throng of all conditions and colors, who tittered and chatted with repressed excitement. There was every conceivable kind of dress there among the contestants, from belted Mother Hubbards to their aristocratic foster-sisters, Empire gowns. There was calico in every design, from polka-dot to Dolly Vardens—and there was—anxiety.

Promptly at ten o'clock the judges, three pompous individuals with white ribbons in their buttonholes, strode in and took their seats just beneath the pulpit. Then there was a short address by the pastor, who, being a wily man and unwilling to put his salry in jeopardy, assured his hearers that if he were one of the judges he would "jest throw up his job an' give a prize to every lady in the room." This brought forth a great laugh and somewhat relieved the nervous tension, but it did not make the real judges feel any better over their difficult task. Indeed, it quite prostrated their chairman, who, in spite of his pompous entrance, sat huddled up in his chair, the sweat breaking out of every pore and the look of final despair in his eyes.

When the pastor was through with his driveling the organist took her place at the wheezy little cabinet organ and struck up a decorous-sounding tune to which the contestants marched round and round the room before the eyes of the bewildered arbiters. They stepped jauntily off, marking the time perfectly to show off their airs and graces as well as their clothing. It was like nothing so much as a sort of religious cake-walk. And the three victims of their own popularity presided over the scene with a solemnity that was not all dignity nor yet pride of place. Five times the contestants marched around and then, at a signal, they halted and ranged themselves in a more or less straight line before the judges.

After careful inspection, somewhat like that of prize cattle at a fair, they were dismissed, and three very nervous and perturbed gentlemen retired to consult.

A Judgment of Paris

Now, these people were lovers of music, and at the very promise that they were to hear their favorite singer, Miss Otilla Bell, they usually became enthusiastic. But to-nignt Miss Bell came out without a greeting, and sang her best without attention. There were other things occupying the minds of the audience. The vocalist was barely done warbling disappointedly when a burst of applause brought a smile to her face. But a glance in the direction toward which every one was looking showed her that the acclamation was not for her, but for the returning judges.

The men took their seats until the handclapping ceased, and then Mr. Hatfield, in sorrowful case, arose to read the committee's report.

"We, de committee——" He paused and looked at the breathless auditors, then went on: "We de committee; I wish to impress dat on you. Dis ain't de decision of one man, but of a committee, an' one of us ain't no mo' 'sponsible den de otah. We, de committee, aftah carefully ezaminin' de costooms of de ladies hyeah assembled ez contestants in dis annual calico social" (It was not annual, but then it sounded well), "do fin'" (Here he cleared his throat again, and repeated himself)— "do fin' dat de mos' strikin' costoom was wo' by Miss Matilda Jenkins, who is daihfo' entitled to de prize."

A little patter of applause came from the Jenkins partisans.

"Will Miss Jenkins please come forward?"

Matilda sidled to the front with well-simulated modesty.

"Miss Jenkins, we, de committee—I repeat, we, de committee, teks great pleasure in pussentin' you wid de prize fu' yo' handsome costoom. It is dis beautiful photygraph a'bum. May you have nuffin' but de faces of frien's in it fu' de reason dat you has no inimies."

He bowed. She bowed. There was again the patter of perfunctory applause, and for that night, at least, the incident was closed.

Fear has second sight, and, albeit he trembled in his shoes, Mr. Hatfield was in nowise astonished when old man Jones called on him next morning at the hotel where he was employed.

"W'y, w'y, how do, Mistah Jones? How do?"

"Howdy?" growled the old man, and went on without pause: "Me an' 'Rilla wants to see you to-night."

"W'y, w'y, Mistah Jones," began Hatfield,

"I—I——" But the other cut him short, his brow gathering.

"Me an' 'Rilla wants to see you," he said.

The scared waiter paused. What should he do? He must decide quickly, for the man before him looked dangerous. There must be no trouble there, because it would mean the loss of his place, and the fact that he was a head waiter was dear to him. Better promise to go and have it out where the presence of Amarilla might mitigate his punishment. So he stammered forth: "'Oh, well, co'se, ef you an' Miss Amarilla wants me, w'y, I'll come."

"All right;" and the irate Jones turned away.

With trembling knees he knocked at the Jones door that night. The old man himself opened to him and received him alone in the front room. This was threatening.

"I reckon you reelizes, Mistah Hatfiel'," said Jones when they had seated themselves and disposed of the weather, "you reelizes dat I had some'p'n putic'lah to say er I wouldn' 'a' had you come hyeah?"

"I knows you's a man o' bus'ness, Mistah Jones."

"I is, suh; so let's come to bus'ness. You

t'ought las' night dat Tildy Jenkins was bettah
dressed den my daughter?"

Hatfield glanced at the glowering face and
stammered: "Well, of co'se, you know, Mistah
Jones, I wasn' de whole committee."

"Don't you try to beat erbout de bush wid
me—answeh my question?" cried the father angrily.

"I don't des see how I kin answeh. You
hyeahed de decision."

"Yes, I hyeahed it, an' I want to know des
what you t'ought."

"Dey was two othah men 'long wid me."

Jones walked over and stood towering before
his trembling victim. "I's gwine to ax you des
once mo', did you t'ink Matildy's dress any put-
tier den my 'Rilla's?"

"No, no—suh," chattered the chairman of the
committee.

"Den," thundered Amarilla's father—"den
you own up dat you showed favoh to one side?"

"No, no—I didn' sho' no favoh—but—but
de majo'ity, hit rules."

"Majo'ity, majo'ity! W'y, w'en I's in de Odd
Fellows' meetin's, ef I's one ag'in fifty, I brings
in a mino'ity repo't."

" 'I'S GWINE TO AX YOU DES ONCE MO' "

A Judgment of Paris

"But I don't reckon dat 'ud 'a' been fittin'."

"Fittin', fittin'! Don't you daih to set thaih an' talk to me erbout fittin', you nasty little rapscallion, you. No, suh! You's shamed my house, you's insulted my gal, an'——"

"Oh, no, Mistah Jones, no. W'y, d'ain't nobody I thinks mo' of den I does of Miss Amarilla."

"Dey hain't, eh? Well, dey's only one way to prove it," said Mr. Jones, sententiously; and then he called: "'Rilla, come hyeah. I'll be right outside de do'," he said, "an' we'll know putty soon how to treat you."

He went out and the vivacious 'Rilla entered.

"Good-evenin'," she said.

"Good-evenin," said Hatfield in agony. "Oh, Miss 'Rilla, Miss 'Rilla," he cried, "I hope you don't think I meant any kin' o' disrespect to you?" She hung her head.

"You know dey ain't nobody dat I think any mo' of den I do of you." In his fervor he took her hand.

"This is so sudden," she said, "but I thought I unnerstood you all along. Ef you really does think so much o' me, I reckon I has to tek you

285

even ef you was sich a naughty boy las' night,"
and she looked at him lovingly.

He stood with staring eyes, dumbfounded.
She had taken his apology for a proposal of marriage, and he—he dared not correct her. He
looked toward the door meditating flight, but remembered what was just behind it.

"Dear Miss Amarilla," he said, "dis is mo'
den I expected."

The ponderous Mr. Jones did not bother them
again that evening. He must have heard all.

Matilda Jenkins first heard the news upon the
street. She came home directly and before taking off her hat picked up the red plush album and
hurled it fiercely out into the yard, where it barely
missed her father's head.

"What's dat?" he cried.

"Dat?" she shrieked. "Dat is de price o'
Mistah Hatfiel'."

SILENT SAM'EL.

Miss Angelina Brown was a young woman of many charms. Every one in Little Africa conceded that. No one who had seen her dash gracefully up the aisle of Mount Moriah Church to the collection-table with tossing head and rustling skirts; no one who had seen her move dreamily through the mazy dance at the hod-carriers' picnics could fail to admit this much. She was a tall, fine-looking girl, with a carriage that indicated that she knew her own worth, as she did.

What added to the glamour that hung about the name of the brown damsel was that she was the only daughter of a very solid citizen—a man who was known to have both "propity" and money. There was no disputing the solidity of the paternal Brown, as there was no question of his utter simplicity and unaffectedness. He had imparted to Angelina a deal of his own good sense, and though she did not flaunt it, she did not, like many others born hitherside the war, disdain the fact that her father had learned on

287

his master's plantation the trade that supported them.

Under these circumstances it is easy to believe that the young woman had many suitors. There were many proper and stylish young men in the community who were willing to take the entrancing girl for herself in spite of the incubus of her riches. Indeed, there were frequent offers of such noble sacrifices; but Angelina was a shrewd high priestess, and she found it better to keep her victims in her train than to immolate them on the altar of matrimony. So it happened that there were few evenings when a light was not visible in the parlor of old Isaac Brown's house, and one or another of the young men of Little 'Africa did not sit there with Angelina.

It was of a piece with the usual good sense that governed this house that slow-going, unpretentious Samuel Spencer—"Silent Sam'el," they called him—made one of these evening sitters. Samuel was a steady-going, good-humored fellow, and a workman under the elder Brown. This may have accounted for Angelina's graciousness to him. For even when he was in her company he had never a word to say for himself, but sat, looked at the lamp, twirled his hat, and smiled. This was certainly not very entertaining for the girl, but then, her father had a high opinion of Samuel's ability. So she would make conversation, and endure his smiles, until old Isaac would call gruffly to him from the kitchen, and he would rise silently and go. Then Angelina was free to entertain whom she pleased for the rest of the evening, for the two men did not part until near midnight.

Once with his employer, Samuel would venture a remark now and then over the something like oily looking tea which they stirred round and round in their glasses. But usually he listened while the old man expounded his new plans and ideas, and every once in a while would shake his head in appreciation, or pat his knee in pure enjoyment. This happened every Wednesday, for that was Samuel's particular evening. Isaac Brown looked forward to it with more pleasure than Angelina. For as he said, when Samuel's silence was referred to, "You needn't say nothin' to me 'bout Sam'el Spencer. I reckon he talks enough fu' me; and 'sides dat, I's allus noticed dat hit took a might' sma't man to know how to keep his mouth shet. Hit's a heap easier to talk."

But there were others who were not so favorably disposed toward old man Brown's "pet," as they called him. Jim White, who was head waiter at the big hotel, and consequently widely conversant with men and things, said: "Huh, ol' Sam go down to ol' man Brown's, an' set up there fur an hour an' a half 'side Miss Angelina, her talkin' an' laughin' an' him lookin' like a bump on a log." And this same joke, though often repeated, never failed to elicit a shout of laughter from the waiters assembled about their leader, and anxious to laugh at anything the autocrat of the dining-room might condescend to say. Others went so far as to twit Samuel himself, but he bore all of this good-naturedly, and without attempting to change his manner, until one memorable night.

It was on the occasion of a great rallying festival at Mount Moriah Church, and a large part of Little Africa was gathered within the church walls, partaking of ice cream, oyster stews and coffee. As Angelina was one of those who had volunteered to help serve the company she had denied herself the pleasure of a "gentleman escort" and had gone early with her father and mother.

Silent Sam'el

Jim White and Samuel Spencer were not the only ones who followed her about that evening with amorous glances. Young men bought oyster stews if she could serve them when they had eaten far beyond their normal capacities. Old men with just teeth enough left to ache gave themselves neuralgia with undesired ice cream.

Jim White had about him a crowd that he treated lavishly every time he could get Angelina's eye; and Samuel himself had already accomplished six oyster stews and was looking helplessly at his seventh.

There is no telling what might have happened had not the refreshments given out and the festival been forced to close. The young men and young women came together in twos and took their way home. But while Angelina stood counting her takings there were no less than six anxious beaus who stood waiting her pleasure.

Of these Sam was the nearest, and those who looked on were about to conclude that even slow as he was he would reach her this time first and gain permission to take her home, when just as a slight sinking of her head showed that her counting was done, Jim White stepped up and, with a bow, asked for "the pleasure." She looked around for a moment and her eye fell on her silent admirer. She hesitated, and then, turning, bowed to White.

The smile died on Sam's face, and he stood watching them blankly. Not until her escort had found her wraps and had put her in them and she had said a light good-night to those who waited did Sam awake from his stupor.

There were some titters as he passed out, and a few remarks such as, "Uh huh, Sam, you too slow fu' Jim. You got to move an' talk faster," or "You sholy was cut out dat time."

But he went on his way, though in spite of the smile that came back to his lips there was a determined look in his eyes. On the church steps he paused and looked after the retreating forms of Angelina and his rival, then with a short but not angry "Huh!" he went his way home.

There was in his mind the consciousness of something wrong, and that something was wrong, his far from dull wits told him, neither with Jim nor Angelina, but himself. He had a perfect right to speak to her first if he could, and she had a right to accept his company. He was bleakly just to every one concerned, and yet he knew by rights he should have taken Angelina home, and then the thought came to him that he could have said nothing to her even had he taken her home. Jim could talk; he couldn't. The knowledge of his own deficiencies overwhelmed him, and he went to bed that night in no happy frame of mind.

For a long while he did not sleep, but lay thinking about Angelina. It was nearly morning when he got suddenly out of bed and began dancing a breakdown in his bare feet, whispering to himself, "By gum, that's it!"

The landlady knocked on the wall to know what was the matter. He replied that he had been attacked with cramp in his feet, but was better now, and so subsided.

From now on a change took place in Samuel's manner of proceeding. The first thing that marked this change was his unexpected appearance in the Brown parlor on the next Monday. Angelina was entertaining another caller, but she received him pleasantly and, so far as an occasional reference to him would suffice, drew him into the conversation. However, he did not stay long, and so his hostess concluded that he had just been passing and had casually dropped in.

What was her surprise when promptly at the same hour on the next night Samuel again came smiling in and settled himself to listen to the talk of that night's caller. Angelina was astounded. What did he mean? Had he begun to spy upon her and her company. Wednesday was his acknowledged night, and of course he had a right to come, but when he turned up on Thursday she openly tossed her head and treated him with marked coldness. The young man who had the pleasure of sitting out the hours on Thursday brought her a bunch of flowers. Samuel was evidently taking lessons, for on Friday night he appeared with a wondrous bouquet.

For one whole week, including Sunday, he was by the side of his divinity some part of every evening. The other young men were provoked. Angelina was annoyed, but less seriously than she might have been when she found that Samuel had the consideration never to stay long. The most joyful one of all concerned was old Isaac Brown himself.

"When Sam'el sets out a cou'tin' he does it jes' like he does evahthing else. Huh, de way he sot his cap fu' Angie is a caution."

But the truth of it was, Samuel Spencer was

deeper than those who knew him could fathom. His week's visit to Angelina had not been without reason or result, and its object might have been discovered as he mumbled to himself on the last night of his constant attendance: "Well, I've heard 'em all talk, but I reckon that little Scott fellow that comes on Friday night's about the slickest of the lot. He'll have to do my talkin' fur me." He chuckled a little, and shook his head solemnly, "Ef somebody else got to speak fur me," he added, "I do' want nothin' but the best talent."

The next week it appeared that Samuel's sudden passion must have burned itself out as suddenly as it had appeared, for not even Wednesday night saw his face in the Brown parlor. Then was Angelina uneasy, for she thought she had offended him; and she didn't want to do that, for he was her father's friend, anyway, even if he was nothing to her, and her father's— oh, well, her father's friend deserved respect. So she instructed the elder Brown to inquire the reason for the young man's sudden defection, and she was greatly soothed, even though she did not care for him, when her parent brought back the message that "Sam'el was all right, an' 'ud be 'roun'."

It was not until Friday night that he came and, contrary to his usual custom, he went directly back into the kitchen, where he spent the hours with the old man. Angelina was piqued, and she tossed her head as he came in just as Mr. Scott was leaving. He sat down and smiled at her for a little while, and then he said abruptly:

"I mean all he said."

She gazed at him in astonishment.

"I mean all he said," he repeated, and soon after bade her good-night.

Friday night after Friday night he came at one hour or another, and after Scott had poured out his heart to Angelina Samuel merely whispered in her ear that he meant all that. Now this was very shrewd of Samuel, for Mr. Scott was a very eloquent and fluent talker, and Angelina thought that if Samuel meant all the other said he must mean a good deal.

One night, with burning words, Scott asked the momentous question. Samuel was in the kitchen with Isaac Brown at the time his rival was making his impassioned plea. Angelina bade her wooer to wait until she had time to and when he had gone she awaited the coming of Samuel.

He came in smiling, as usual.

"I mean all he said," he asserted.

"How do you know, you do? You do' know what he said," retorted Angelina.

"I mean all he said," repeated Sam.

"La, Mr. Spencer, you are the beatenes' man! If you mean all he said, why don't you say it yo'se'f?"

"I can't," said Sam simply.

"Well, Mr. Scott surely has said enough tonight."

"I mean all he said."

"I'm mighty 'fraid you'll want to back out when you hear it."

"I mean all he said," and Sam laid an emphasis on the "all." He was slowly working his way toward Angelina. His wits began to tell him what Scott had said.

"You ain't never ast me what he said."

"What?"

"Oh, I can't tell you; don't you know?"

By this time he had reached her and put his arm around her trim waist.

"I mean all he said."

"Well, then, I says yes to you fur what you means, even if you won't say it," and Angelina ducked her head on his breast.

Sam's eyes shone, and it was a good deal later before he left that night. As he stood at the gate he suddenly broke his silence and said, "I thought Scott was nevah goin' to git to the question."

THE WAY OF A WOMAN.

Any man who has ever wooed in earnest, or thought so, knows how hard it is to have his suit repulsed time and time again. However the capricious one may smile at times, one "no" upsets the memory of many days of smiles.

The structure of Gabe Harris' hopes had fallen so often that he had begun to build it over again listlessly and mechanically enough, until one momentous day, when it seemed fallen for good.

He had come by, as usual, upon his cart that evening after work, and paused, as was his wont, for a chat with his desired one, Anna Maria Moore. He had been hard at work all day hauling from the clay-pits, and so was not a thing of beauty as to clothes. But if Anna Maria loved him—and he believed she did—love was blind, which left him all right in his own eyes and hers.

Perhaps he was right even thus far, and all would have gone well had not the plump, brown beauty of the girl overcome him as he stood chatting with her.

The realization of her charms, of her desirableness, swept over him with a rush of emotion. Instinctively he held out his arms to her. They were in the front yard, too. "W'en—w'en you gwine ma'y me, honey? Tell me."

Anna Maria froze at once. She grew as rigid as the seams in her newly starched calico.

"W'y—w'y, what's de mattah, Anna Maria?" stammered the discomfited Gabe.

" 'Scuse me, Mistah Ha'is," said the lady, with dignity, "but I's not in de habit ob bein' spoke to in dat mannah."

"W'y, what's I done, Anna Maria?"

"What's you done, sah? What's you done? W'y you's scandalized me 'fo' de eyes ob de whole neighbo'hood," and the calico swished itself as well as its stiffness would allow into the house.

Gabe scratched his head. "Well, I'll be dad-burned!" he ejaculated.

Just then Uncle Ike, Anna Maria's father, came up. He was Gabe's friend and ally, and the young fellow's bewilderment was not lost upon him.

"What's de mattah, Brothah Gabe?" he questioned.

"W'y, Unc' Ike, I done axed Anna Maria to

ma'y, an' she say I's insulted an' scandalized de neighbo'hood. Huccome dat?"

"Tsch, tsch, tsch, Brothah Gabe; you sholy doesn't knew de pherlosophy ob oomankin'."

"I reckon I ain't up on dat, Unc' Ike; seems I ain' had de spe'ence dat hab fell to yo' lot."

The present was Uncle Ike's fourth matrimonial venture, and he was supposed to know many things. He went on: "Now, Brothah Gabe, in co'tin' a ooman, less'n she's a widdah ooman, dey's th'ee t'ings you got to do; you got to satisfy huh soul, you got to chawm huh yeah, an' you got to please huh eye. 'Tain't no use doin' one ner tothah less'n you does all—dat is, I say, pervided it ain't a widdah lady; dey bein' easiah to please an' mo' unnerstannin' laik. Well, you come hyeah, aftah yo' day's wo'k, an' you talk to Anna Maria. She know you been a'wo'kin', an'll mak' a good pervider; dat satisfy huh soul."

"Yes, suh; she smile w'en I was a-talkin' to huh, an' dat what mak me fu'git myse'f."

"Uh-huh," said the old man, wagging his head sagely and stroking the straggling beard upon his chin, "uh-huh, dat mean dat you chawm huh yeah; but hol' on, hol' on dey's one mo' t'ing. How in de name ob common sense you spec' to please huh eye a-comin' hyeah in sich togs ez deze? Ki yi, now you see."

Again Gabe had recourse to his signal of perplexity, and woolly head and grimy nails came together in a half-hearted scratch.

"Unc' Ike, you sholy hab opened my eyes," he said, as he went slowly out to his cart.

On the morrow he arrayed himself in his best, and hitching his mare to a buggy not yet too rickety to awe some of his less prosperous neighbors, started toward the home of his inamorata. Old Suke, accustomed to nothing lighter than her cart on workdays, first set her ears doubtfully at the unaccustomed vacation, and then, seeming to realize that it was really a vacation, a gala-day, she tossed her head and stepped out bravely.

In the heart of Gabe Harris a similar exultation was present. What now would check him in his quest of the fair one? He had fulfilled all the requirements laid down by Uncle Ike, and Uncle Ike knew. He had already satisfied her soul; he had done his duty as to "chawmin' her yeah," now he went forth a potential conqueror for the last great feat—the pleasing of her eyes. Gone were the marks and the memory of the clay-pits, gone was the ashiness of dust from his hardened hands. His self-abashing cap was replaced by an agressive "stiff hat," while his black coat and waistcoat, with drab trousers, completed an invincible make-up.

It was an autumn day, the year was sighing toward its close, but there was a golden touch in the haze that overhung the mean streets where he passed, and somewhere up in a balsam poplar a bird would persist in singing, and something in Gabe's heart kept answering, answering, as he alighted and hitched Suke before Anna Maria's gate.

A little later she came out arrayed in all her glory. She passed through the gate which the smiling Gabe held open for her, and stepped lightly into the buggy. Suke turned one inquisitive glance over her shoulder, and then, winking slowly to herself, consented to be unhitched and to jog leisurely toward the country roads. What Gabe said to Anna Maria and what Anna Maria said to Gabe on that drive is not recorded. But it is evident that the lover had been preparing his lady for something momentous, for upon returning late that afternoon he paused as he helped her alight, and whispered softly: "I got sompin' mo' to say to you."

As they entered the house, the smell of baking biscuits and of frying pork assailed their nostrils. Aunt Hannah Moore also had recognized this as a gala-day, and was putting herself out to lay such a feast for her daughter's suitor as he should remember for many a day to come. Gabe sat down in the spick-and-span front room.

"Ma's biscuits cert'n'y does smell scan'lous," Anna Maria commented, agreeably.

Gabe's mind was too full of his mission to heed the remark. The momentous second had arrived —the second that held the fruition of all his ambitions, all his dreams. He plumped down on his knees at her feet. "Oh, Anna Maria," he cried, "Anna Maria, ain't you gwine hab me now?"

Anna Maria turned on him a look full of startled surprise, which soon turned to anger and disdain. "Look hyeah, Gabe," she said, wrathfully, "what's de mattah wid you? Is you done tuk leab ob yo' senses? Ain't you got no 'spect fo' a lady's feelin's? Heah I's tiahed and hongry, an' you come 'roun talkin' sich foolishness ez dat. No, I ain't gwine hab you. Git up f'om daih, an' ac' sensible. I's hongry, I is."

Gabe got up sheepishly, dusting his knees.

Anna Maria turned to the window. He took his hat, and let himself out of the door.

"Heyo, Brothah Gabe, wha you gwine? You ain't gwine 'way fo' suppah, am you? We got som monstous fine middlin' daih fryin' speshly fo' you," was the greeting from Anna Maria's father.

"D'you want to buy Suke? I's gwine 'way f'om hyeah."

"What's de mattah'd you?" was the old man's quick question.

"I's done filled all de 'quirements you tol' me, an' axed Anna Maria 'gain, an' she won't hab me, an' I's gwine 'way."

"No, y'ain't. Set down."

Gabe seated himself beside his adviser.

"W'en you ax Anna Maria?"

"Jes' now."

"Oomph, oomph, oomph," said the old man, reflectively; and he went on: "Gabe, fo' a ha'd-wo'kin, money-savin', long-haided man you sholy has got less sense dan anybody I know."

"What's I done now?" said Gabe, disconsolately. "Ain't I filled all de 'quirements? Ain't I satisfied huh soul? Aain't I chawmed huh

yeah? Ain't I pleased huh eye? Now wha' mo'
—oh, 'tain't no use!"

"Hol' on, hol' on, I say; you done all dese
t'ings. You's satisfied huh soul, you's chawmed
huh yeah, you's pleased huh eye, an' she's jes
ready fo' you, but Lawd a' massy 'pon me, ain't
you got mo' sense dan to pop de question to a
lady w'en she hungry? Gabe, you got lots to
l'arn."

" 'Tain't no use, Unc' Ike; ef she eat suppah
an' git satisfied, den she ain't gwine need me."

"You set down an' wait till aftah suppah, I
say."

Just then the call for supper came, and Gabe
went in with the black Solomon. During the
blessing Anna Maria was cold and distant, but
when the first biscuit was passed to her her face
brightened. She half smiled as she broke it open
and filled its hot interior with rich yellow butter.
The smile was on full force when she had tasted
the brown crisp "middlin'," and by the time she
had the "jackets" off two steaming potatoes her
face was beaming.

With wonder and joy Gabe watched the meta-
morphosis take place, and Uncle Ike had con-

stantly to keep nudging or kicking him under the table to keep him from betraying himself.

When the supper was done, and it went on to a merry ending, Aunt Hannah refused Anna Maria's help with mock fierceness, and Uncle Ike went out on the porch to smoke. Only the front room was left for Anna Maria and Gabe, and thither they went.

Gabe lingered for awhile on the brink, and then plunged in: "Anna Maria, I's failed, an' failed, an' I's waited an' waited. Is you—is you —will you have me now?"

"La, Gabe Ha'is, you is de beatenes'!" But her hand slipped into his.

"Is you gwine have me, Anna Maria?" he repeated.

"I reckon I'll have to," she said.

Out on the porch Uncle Ike waited long in the silence; then he said: "Well, dat's a moughty good sign, but it sholy time fu' it. Oomph, oomph, oomph, 'oomen an' colts, an' which is de wus, I don' know."